Forbidden

An Erotic Collection of Short Stories

A Temptation Press
Anthology

Forbidden

An Erotic
Collection

Forbidden

An Erotic Collection of Short Stories

A Temptation Press Anthology

For permission requests, write to the publisher:
"Attention: Permissions Coordinator"
Temptation Press
PO Box 1172
Union Lake, Michigan 48387
mail to: info@TemptationPress.com

© 2019 Temptation Press – An Imprint of Zimbell House Publishing
Published in the United States by Temptation Press

This book is rated for 18+

All Rights Reserved

Trade Paper ISBN: 978-1-64390-020-9
.mobi ISBN: 978-1-64390-021-6
ePub ISBN: 978-1-64390-022-3
Library of Congress Control Number: 2019901368

First Edition: February 2019
10 9 8 7 6 5 4 3 2 1

Acknowledgments

Temptation Press would like to thank all those that contributed to this anthology. We chose to showcase six new voices that best embodied our vision for this work.

We would also like to thank all those on our Temptation Press team for all their hard work and dedication to these projects.

Contents

Distracted

Caycie Thompson

The afternoon sun is lazy in the sky. It hangs there beating down its rays on the gray cement below. Unrelenting. Cruel.

I sit, watching the passersby attend to their errands below me. So bored, preoccupied. Lonely. I wonder what they think about as they bustle along. Do they think, or is it that they move, almost on autopilot, from chore to chore?

It is hot—too hot for an autumn day—but I guess this is what they are referring to when they talk about global warming.

I hear my name and turn my head to the sound. A chill runs up my spine. He's here. The baritone of his voice plays on my skin. I try to play coy, but my body betrays me. I have no choice but to react.

He approaches, and I drink him in, the whole of his powerfully built frame, just over six feet. His brown hair cut short, and playful eyes a blue-green in color. His lopsided smile conveys more than a little mischief.

I turn away from him. I don't want to give away how he affects me. My breath has become shallow, and my pulse has quickened with anticipation. Will he touch me? I'm torn. I'm desperate for his touch, and though I have never known it, I know that if he doesn't touch me, I will surely die.

I don't have to wait long. I sense that he is near me. He closes the distance between us with a few short strides. I feel his breath on the nape of my neck. His scent masculine, patchouli, musk and a touch of sweat. He is earthy and delicious.

His breath is hot on my neck as he steps next to me and his hand slides down my arm to my fingers. We entwine them, and he draws our combined hands along my lithe form. He traces my waist to my skirt, which rests mid-thigh. Our fingers burn my naked thigh as he delicately traces the hem. His body presses into mine, and I feel his yearning.

I turn to face him, my lips parted in anticipation of his mouth. When our lips meet, his are soft and moist. His breath is hot as he claims my lips for his own and I melt into his grasp.

His arms encircle me, and I feel small, vulnerable. Protected. Worshipped.

His hands slide effortlessly across my body as the need rises between us. His lips leave mine, and I am breathless.

My fingers fumble with the buttons of his shirt as I try desperately to read the heat of him. I pull off his belt as he helps me out of my shirt. My knees are weak as he kisses my neck. His tongue traces a line to my ear lobe and kisses his way back down to the exposed flesh of my shoulder, the valley of my neck, and I watch in excited frustration as he gently encircles each beast in turn. First the right, then the left, he covers them with gentle, loving kisses. The tickle of his five o'clock shadow on my tender skin is almost too much to bear. I must have him.

I unzip his jeans, and it is clear that he too feels the urgency. Strong hands caress the swell of my buttocks. His thumbs hook under the thin lace of my panties and pull them down. They lay discarded on the floor—the last barrier to what we need.

His muscular arms raise me up to his waist's height. I look down into his eyes. They are no longer playful, they are focused and full of desire. I lean down and capture his lips in a passionate kiss. The top of my tongue touches his and desire, like an electric current, courses through me anew. Held securely in his powerful grasp he braces me against the wall.

Shifting beneath me I feel his rigid manhood against me for only a moment. He presses forward, and I gasp. My eyes open in surprised delight.

We are one.

I cry out in joy as he takes me. I cling to him as my body sings out praises with every thrust of his hips. I am merely an instrument and he the gifted musician.

As we build to a beautiful crescendo, sweat mists our bodies. We belong to one another, and he whispers my name. His voice is thick with desire. The sound is all I need to send me over the edge—to crest the wall into delirium. I call out to him, so lost in the throes of passion, I am sure he cannot hear me. He feels me though, of this I am certain. He falters once and cries out.

Breathing heavily, sighing, laughing, he sets me down. My long brown hair, usually so neatly tied back is loose and wild, clinging to my face in sweaty pieces. He stands before me, his shirt unbuttoned and damp, his chest muscles glistening. A bead of sweat trails down the hills of his pecs to his navel. I trace the line, drawing my finger along the river of our combined dampness.

We catch our breath and know that we only have a few moments before our colleagues will enter the conference room. We dress in silence, and he steals away to his post.

I am hooked. I knew I would be.

The masterful way he held my body. How attentive he was to my needs. I must have him again. I wondered if he too were thinking of the next time, because there was no doubt, there would be a next time.

I shift in my seat, the gusset of my panties damp, my nipples straining against my blouse.

"Hey. Are you okay? You look flushed."

Someone is talking to me. I bring my attention back to the room, dragging my eyes from the process servers and workaday schlubs on the grey cement below.

"Hmmm? Yes," I say. "I must have been daydreaming." I look up guiltily. I should at least pretend to be paying attention.

I meet his eye across the conference room table. Does he know? Can he read my mind? Does he have any idea how delicious it would be? Deftly, I glide my tongue across my lower lip. A glint of recognition forms in his eye.

I squeeze my thighs together delighting in the dangerous pressure, glance down at my wedding ring and sigh.

Who said business meetings were boring?

I return to my corner office and close the door. Something has to be done about this. He seems to be everywhere, and it is getting so hard to look at him. It is getting so wet, to be more specific.

He created this fire inside me that was becoming hard to deny. The way he looked at me during the meeting, it was as though we shared the same fantasy.

I had to stop thinking about him. There was work to do. Burying myself in work was the solution. But then the thought of him burying his face between my parted thighs came to mind. My breath hitched in my chest as I imagined him burying his tongue between my folds.

My hand slips down my body, molding my clothes to my overheated flesh. I reach my treasure trove. My eyes flick toward the door to ensure it is locked.

It would not look good if the Chief Information Officer were caught with her hand in the cookie jar. Especially when the cookie jar held delights far more satisfying than an Oreo.

It is far too risky to be doing this in my office, but there is no turning back now. I have to make sure that when the moment hits, I can stifle my cry. Sensation after sensation crashes through my mind as I picture his young, luscious body positioned below mine, his mouth busily bringing me nearer and nearer to climax.

My finger strums firmly across my too-sensitive button, and I soar. Quickly I bring my hand to my mouth to cut off the sound. The sound of panting fills the enclosed office. My orgasm is short lived but powerful. I sit in my high-back leather chair and try to catch my breath.

I have to stop doing this at work. Someone is bound to walk in one of these days. Still, it has been too long since I have had a man touch me the way I need to be touched.

There was an otherness to being a widow. People did not seem to know what to say to you. The first year was incredibly difficult. I had become so isolated. With the kids gone off to school and their own lives, I was very much on my own. For a long time that was all right. I took care of myself, ate right, exercised—all of the things you are supposed to do. I had even tried to get back out there once or twice at the unsubtle urging of girlfriends, but I wasn't ready to give up that place in my heart that was reserved for my husband.

It wasn't until Charlie started at my firm that I had felt remotely interested in a man, and what I felt for him was far more than interest. He lit a fire in me that kept me awake at night. I thought that those days were long behind me, though only being fifty-one I don't know why I had rationalized it that way.

He was a magnificent specimen, tall, and finely built. An exceptional IT professional, he was a man who specialized in security, and I admired his intellect. Despite all that, it was his strong hands, his carefully groomed five o'clock shadow and his sculptured shoulders that held my attention when he came into the room. I watched him while he spoke, embarrassed to admit that I rarely heard what he said as I was captivated by the curve of his sensuous lips. I often thought of those lips on my body. My lips on his body. He made me wet.

There was only one problem—he was only a couple of years older than my son.

I fix my skirt and give myself a once over before I open my office door. I walk to the washroom and stare into the mirror at my reflection. My hair hangs in tight curls and frames my still flushed face. I wash my hands and pat my face with a cool, damp paper towel. There are only a couple of hours left until the end of the day. I can make it.

Once I return to my office, I pour myself a glass of water and turn my attention back to my monitor.

A sharp rap at the door pulls my eyes from the email I had been reading.

"Come in," I call. Charlie's supervisor, Loretta, stands in the doorway. "Hey, Loretta. What's up?"

"I was just wondering when you needed the reports pulled for the incidents we attended to over the month."

Loretta pauses for a moment and then continues. I suppose the look on my face is enough to convey to her that I had no idea to what she referred.

"In the meeting," she began. "The director wanted reports from each sector to send up to headquarters." Loretta twists her mouth impatiently.

I hate when she does that. "Right," I respond. "Um, if I could get them first thing tomorrow that would be great. I have a one-on-one meeting with her tomorrow at ten o'clock."

"That would mean that someone would have to stay tonight to get it done."

"Yes, Loretta, I suppose it would."

"Okay, well, I am not able to stay tonight to assist with this project. I guess I will canvas my team to see who is available to work this evening."

"Yes, that would be good. If you could find one or two people to work tonight, it would be greatly appreciated."

"Sure, I will ask. But I would be surprised if I could find two." Loretta said dismissively and walks out of the room.

"Thank you, Loretta," I said to her receding form and turn back to my monitor. I shake my head at the interaction. She could be a lot to handle, but she was a good tech.

The remainder of the day had passed by quickly and without incident.

A knock on my door brought my attention to my doorway. This time it was not Loretta's perpetually disappointed face looking back at me. A warm smile spread across my lips.

"Hi, guys!" I said, with probably a little too much excitement in my voice. In my door stood Pamela and Charlie.

"Hey Boss," Pamela said. "We heard you were looking for volunteers to stay to help get those reports out?"

"Yeah. You're both available?" I asked. I fixed my eyes on Pamela as I was afraid my eagerness would betray me if I caught Charlie's eye.

"Well, I am free for an hour or so—I have to take off after that. Charles here, on the other hand, is at your disposal. All night if need be," Pamela responded, and shot Charlie a quick look and then rested her gaze on me.

Was I mistaken? Did she just make a comment laced with innuendo? I can't be that out of touch to have missed it, and I thought I saw Charlie's cheeks flush a bit. I wouldn't dare acknowledge it.

"Okay! That's great," I said. "Well, there's no shortage of data to pull and organize, so let's get started, shall we?"

Pamela came into my office a short time later to say that she was leaving but that her analytics were complete. She placed her report on my desk and walked out of my office. She turned back and said, "I'll send Charlie in, so you two can make sure you are on the same page."

Okay, what was that about? Had she seen the way I was looking at him in the meeting earlier? I had always been so careful around him. I didn't want to look like a cougar ready to pounce on a younger man. I hoped Charlie didn't see it that way.

Charlie came into my office about fifteen minutes later. He had a report in his hand as well.

"Done for the night?" I asked. I hoped that he wasn't, but I wouldn't make him stay if he wanted to leave.

"No, I just wanted to give you this before I started to work on the last one."

"Oh. Okay. No problem." There was a strange energy in the room.

Charlie placed the report on my desk and lingered there for a moment. I looked at the folder and his hand. The thickness of his fingers and how they so innocently perched on the folder. I was entranced by them.

I looked up to see he was watching me curiously. He had the same look that graced his face at the meeting.

"Uh, how about we order some dinner in? We might be here a while yet." My offer was selfish, but it might entice him to stay a bit longer.

"Dinner sounds great."

Charlie sat down in the chair opposite my desk. His brown eyes fixed on mine. I felt a familiar heat rising within me. If he only knew what he did to me.

"I want to apologize for Pam's comments earlier. I could see that they made you a little bit uncomfortable, and who knows what she said when she was in here earlier." Charlie laughed.

Was he nervous? Around me? He had never acted that way before.

"I wasn't uncomfortable. A little innuendo never hurt anybody. Pamela's just like that I guess," I chuckled in response. "Okay, so, what shall we have for dinner?"

I stand up and walk around my desk. Charlie is watching my every move. He is the one prowling. I can hardly believe it.

As I walk past him, he shifts subtly in his chair. The back of his hand grazes my leg as I pass. I slow for a moment, then continue to the cabinet where I keep the menus.

He stands and joins me at the cabinet and takes the stack from my hand. He places them on the round table where, in the morning, I would have the meeting with my boss. He's so close to me. The smell of his cologne overpowers rational thought. I turn to face him, my body teeming with desire.

"I hope I am not out of line when I say I saw that look you gave me in the conference room today. I liked it."

"Oh?"

"Yeah."

I shudder as Charlie slides his hand up my arm and pulls me closer to him. My chest is pressed to his. His hand turns my face to his, and his lips graze mine.

"I have wanted to do this for a long time. It wasn't until today that I knew you felt the same way."

I feel his lips slide sensuously over mine as he speaks. My knees are weak as he continues.

"I have been craving an opportunity like this for a long time. To be alone with you. Pamela knows that. Hence the comments earlier. I hope this is not too forward, but I haven't been able to think of anything else since the meeting today."

Before I can respond, Charlie slides his tongue along my bottom lip. I melt into his embrace and part my lips to allow him access. He draws me closer in his arms and backs me up to the cabinet. My mind is rushing. I can feel the heat from his body radiating from him like a furnace. I kiss him back. I stroke my tongue along the bottom of his. The tips of our tongues clash together. The sound of my soft whimpers fills my office. My hands slide down his body. They are urgent and seeking more. I am too hot to consider romance. I need him inside me. I need him to pleasure me.

Without speaking, he recognizes my craving. His hands reach under my skirt and slip one finger along the lacey material of my panties to the soaked cotton. A groan of approval echoes in his throat. I sigh and lean my head back as he tastes the delicate skin of my neck. His finger slips past the cotton and gently sweeps along my sensitive swollen lips. He turns me toward the couch and gently guides me onto my back. I watch, entranced, as he pushes my skirt up—the material gathered at my waist— and he lays heated kiss upon kiss up the suppleness of my thighs.

He draws my panties down. My neatly trimmed mound is exposed to his gaze, his touch. With deft fingers, he explores. His fingers become slippery as they slide through my wetness.

He leans forward, and I hold my breath. When his lips finally touch me, I am in heaven. He draws one lip in at a time, sucking for a moment and then onto the next. His tongue taps the root of my heat. He pushes my thighs apart and holds them firmly. He attaches his suckling lips to my clit and holds on. Pleasure bursts through me. I feel my orgasm rushing forward. I cannot hold back. My fingers comb through his hair.

"Charlie," I whimper. Calling his name makes him hotter to me. I try to close my thighs around his head, but his arms hold me open to his delicious assault. He begins to flick my clit with his tongue and stars dance before my eyes.

"I'm coming," I cry. My fingers, entwined in his hair, hold him tightly. My breath comes in short, intense gasps as his tongue ravishes my delicate button. His face is drenched from the amount of juice my pussy produced in response to his masterful touch. I can barely catch my breath.

My eyes blink open. Charlie is standing naked before me, his swollen cock proudly before him. I could not have imagined a more perfect sight. I lick my lips and raise up on my elbows. He is beautiful. My imagination does not do justice to his physique. The peaks and valleys of his muscular arms, the breadth of his shoulders, the happy trail that leads from his belly button to his fabulously thick manhood.

I stand and wrap my hand around his thickness. I can feel his heartbeat in the meaty tool, and I can no longer wait to feel it crash through my gates and bring me to the peaks of pleasure. Luckily for me, Charlie seems to be one step ahead.

Kissing me passionately, I taste myself on his lips. Spicy and tart. I push my skirt down over my hips and fight with the buttons on my shirt to remove it. Charlie expertly unhooks my bra, and my breasts spill forth.

Leaning me against the table, he brings his mouth down to my nipples in turn, sucking them and playfully biting them to long, hard peaks.

Without warning, Charlie turns me around. His face buries in my tight curls, and I feel his hardness across my buttocks. A trail of precum marks his sensuous path. I lean forward on the table and part my thighs. Murmuring to him, he positions himself between my quaking thighs.

"Take me," I utter. I feel him slide the bloated head along my pouting lips and slowly enter me. I gasp as I feel him slip inside. He moves slowly as he sinks inch after inch into my burning honeypot. My pussy ripples around his hard cock as each inch of him causes mini orgasms to shoot through me.

He pulls back just as slowly, and I don't know how much of this delicious torture I can take. His strokes are so deliberate. I can only mewl my approval, I have lost the ability to speak.

His left hand strokes my hip and grabs my leg. He raises my ankle to his hip and holds it there. I suck in a deep breath as he bottoms out inside me, his balls resting on my engorged clit. His right hand holds my right hip, and I feel him draw back. I cry out as he slams into me. His hand on my hip holds me in place, while his other hand holds me open. I feel his balls tickle my clit on every stroke. His cock brushing against my g-spot causes my knee to buckle, but he holds me tighter bringing me quickly to an earth-shattering release. My cunt squeezes him, and I hear his breath quickening. His pace is unrelenting as he comes closer. The sound of our bodies slapping together is music. My soaking pussy sucking on his dick urges him to release, and he cries out. The warm splashes deep inside me, the feeling of his strong hands holding me, of the intense sensation my clit was experiencing thrust me into another mind-blanking orgasm.

My body shudders beneath him as he lays on top of me, our orgasms subsiding. As Charlie pulls out, my nerve endings light up anew, and I smile.

Turning around, I kiss him. I draw a finger along his wet and sticky cock and bring it to my lips.

"We had better order some food. It's gonna be a long night."

I was right about one thing in my daydream. Without a doubt, there would be a next time.

Getting Wet

Gina Durden

Jesse could hardly see where he was. Moisture hung so densely in the air that it gathered in drops, then streaked down the windshield. He flicked on the wiper every now and then to clear it. Georgia was damned wet. And hot—nothing like the arid summers in Topeka. Jesse rolled the window down, and water trickled off the sill and onto his jeans. Moist air rushed into his nose and lungs, and he had an involuntary feeling he could drown in this air. It wasn't even raining. So much moisture was suspended in the air that it precipitated out as mist. Under every street lamp, a cone of iridescent drops caught the yellow light and bounced it around, making the haze even brighter.

He'd been driving around Savannah since ten last night. His now wet watch said two. His clothes were soggy. Even his bones felt wet. Cobbled streets jostled the car and his head and his stomach. Too much beer. Where all that great blues was hiding, he hadn't been able to figure out. Nor, where any hot southern women were holed up. He flicked the knob on the radio. News. Nixon was selling some new lie. They still hadn't figured out how to win that damned war. When the music came back on it was some kind of hard rock. The silence was better.

The waterfront was the only place there might be a breeze. He headed there. Endless old houses rolled by on either side—mansions and row houses—not far apart from each other but with different lives inside. Dreamers, sleeping through the heat if they could. Street signs were coated with moisture and reflections from the headlights made them illegible. He finally recognized the street that ran down to the riverfront, not by the street sign, but by the huge live oaks that guarded it. He turned at the last minute.

The car skidded on the slick road, bounced in and out of a pothole, and righted itself just in time, but when Jesse looked up, he was headed right for a figure kneeling on the sidewalk.

"Jesus H—"

He pumped the brakes and steered to miss her, but she jumped up and ran, getting more in his way than she was on the sidewalk. Jesse braked hard and stopped. The girl stood in his headlights, shaking and drenched, wrapped in what looked like a blanket.

He got out. It had started to rain in earnest now, and he could see she was getting soaked.

"Hey, you all right?" he called.

She said nothing, just shivering in the warm rain and looking at him with big scared eyes.

"Come on. I don't know where I can take you, but you can sit in the car. Get dry." He motioned her to him, but she stood staunchly. A stranger on a dark wet night. Sure, she'd jump right in with him and get dragged off who knew where.

"It's okay," he said. "I'm not going to hurt you." *Believe me,* he suggested silently, *trust your instincts.* He smiled and held out his arms to show welcome or comfort, then walked over closer to see if she would run away.

"You're soaked, and I'm getting that way fast. Come on. Let me help you."

She slumped, seeming to relent to whatever misery came next. A slim hand reached up and brushed away a mass of dark hair. Underneath a pale face stared back at him, frightened, weary. *What could have happened to this girl?* It looked like she wasn't going to bolt, and he thought he might steer her to the car. He put out a hand, and although she didn't take it, she came willingly enough.

She almost tripped on the draped material, and he took hold of her. His hands on her arms and shoulders sensed the almost birdlike lightness of her. He opened the passenger side, sat her on the seat, lifted her thin dripping legs into the car and shut the door. He scrambled inside too, relishing at once the dry space, shedding his soaked shirt for the barely drier t-shirt underneath.

"You should get out of those wet clothes. And you're all muddy." He took in the dripping dirty wrap. "You're really messing up this rental car. I'll get charged for it for sure." He reached over and tried to lift the soggy fabric from one shoulder, but she grabbed the cloth and pulled it even tighter. He withdrew.

"What the hell happened to you?"

She said nothing.

"Like you might want to tell me—a complete stranger." He felt compelled to talk to make up for her silence. "Well, you can just sit there. I was headed for the river, but there's no reason to go now. I guess I'll have to figure something out to get us both out of this mess."

The pattering of rain on the roof of the car had become loud enough to dampen any conversation, one-way as it was. Jesse started the engine.

The girl glanced up as if asking, 'what now?' Her focus ranged from him to the road ahead and back.

"Look, I don't know what's happened to you, but both of us need to get dry. I'm going to take you back to my motel room. Don't get all scared. It's the only place I know in this damned swamp, so that's where we're going. Just hold tight and ..."

Just as the car started to move, she grabbed the door handle and flung the door open in a flash.

He didn't think she could move that fast. He grabbed her arm, so light and thin he was afraid it might snap in his hand. Hands that were more used to rope and cattle than young girls. A cowboys' hands. He could hurt her. "Hey, now, don't go getting all scared. I won't hurt you. I promise." He had braked and grabbed her so quickly that he was stopped smack in the middle of an empty street. Jesse reached across her and shut the car door. The gutters ran with rippling water, and the rain had not let up. "Am I going to have to tie you up, girl?

I'm just trying to help, for Christ's sake. Look, if you have somewhere else you can go, just tell me and I'll take you there instead." He stared at her, waiting to see how the rest of this long night was going to go.

"No," she said quietly, tucking her head and shaking it once. Still, she was pressed against the door, as near to out as she could get.

"No mother? No father?"

She shook her head again.

"No boyfriend, no husband?"

She shook it again even harder.

"Then I guess we have no choice. You try that door again, and I'll tie you up like a calf at branding time. You hear me?"

She nodded and wrapped herself tighter in her soggy cocoon.

Jesse drove down the highway out of town, headed for the motel room like a cow for the barn at feeding time, going as fast as he dared, hoping to discourage her from trying to run again. He hated having to make threats like that to the girl, scare her even more. But she could hurt herself.

When they finally got to his motel, he had to unstick her from the car seat, and then she almost passed out in his arms. He ended up carrying her to the door and propping her against him as he fumbled for the key to let them in. She was still dripping and muddy. Jesse settled her in a chair and made sure she wouldn't fall over. Then he sat on the end of the bed and contemplated the situation.

He'd come to Savannah to make a business deal but stayed to take in what he'd been told was some great blues. He must have hit the musical low point because every place he'd tried was closed or the regular band was not playing. *Everybody must take off when it gets like this,* he thought, *hot and wet – muggy, they called it around here. Word suits.* He thought the night couldn't have got worse, and now here he was in the middle of a god damned mess with a drowned teen. He eyed the wet girl-sized bundle dripping on the chair.

"Look here," he said to her. "You got to get dry. You want me to do this, or can you stand up on your own?"

"I can stand up," she said in a piping voice, hesitating. "I think. I ran so far. I didn't know where I was. And then it started to rain." She looked up at him shyly. Her voice was high, childlike and had the soft drawl of the coast. Her eyes were brown, the color of a calf's. She sucked in a big wet gasp. "I can't take this off in front of you."

"So, you go in the bathroom and get washed up. And then we'll get you into something warm. I might have an extra shirt and some shorts you can wear. Just get in there and when you're cleaned up let me know and I'll pass you some clothes."

She stood, wobbled a bit and slowly made her way across the room, leaving muddy tracks and trailing what Jesse now realized was a big white sheet. Her pale legs spread it open as she walked. Naked underneath. *That was why she wouldn't let me remove it in the car,* he thought. And when you run off in a sheet, it's not because you're alone in bed. Some man had been responsible for her state.

She did as told. Jesse passed her a pair of boxer shorts and a tee shirt through the bathroom door and got her settled, dry and warm, under the covers at last. With her taking up the bed, he wondered where in this nearly bare room he might land for some rest. Suddenly he was dead tired and still hadn't showered. He left her asleep in the bed to go clean up. The sheet was still on the bathroom floor. He picked it up and took it in the shower with him thinking to rinse off the mud. Turning it in his hands, he stopped suddenly. There was blood. Not a lot. He flashed back to his first time with a girl and the spot they'd had to wash out before her mother changed the sheets and found it.

When he returned, she was on her side turned away from the center of the bed, out like a light. Maybe she wouldn't notice if he just lay beside her for a few minutes. He eased down on the near side of the bed and had one single thought before he was asleep—*too bad she had to find out about sex this way.*

When Jesse woke, the girl was sitting up cross-legged on the bed beside him, looking hard at him with a frown on her face. Her dark hair had dried to a soft brown. Her frightened eyes had softened. His mouth tasted like cotton, and he had a morning hard-on poking up under the thin cotton of his shorts. She was looking at that too.

"I guess I owe you some kind of explanation," she said, her I's sounding like soft "ahs."

"Honey, you don't owe me a thing. You were about to drown out there." He sat up against the headboard and pulled a handful of loose coverlets over his tenting shorts. "Don't you have any family? Surely your daddy didn't let you out on a night like this with a boy like …" He halted.

"My daddy left us for another woman. My mother works nights in a motel on Tybee Island. We live halfway between Savannah and there. There's no buses this time of night, and I didn't know anybody to go to where my Mama wouldn't have found out. If I get home before nine. I'll be okay. Mama has to take the bus home, and it's usually on time, or late. Never early."

"What were you doing out like that. What happened?" He almost stopped. What did he need with this girl's drama? But he couldn't help himself. "I saw the sheet. That wasn't a nosebleed."

She actually blushed. Then she recovered and put up a front.

"It was my own fault. I guess I just don't know what men want."

"Wait a minute. If some asshole popped your cherry against your will, it wasn't your fault." He heard himself and stopped. "Sorry, that's not how it's done, sweetheart. Real men are not rapists."

"But I asked for it. I mean, I was just so sick to death of being a virgin. Here I am already a sophomore and almost twenty-one. All my friends are telling me they've done it, and how great it is and I've watched girls making out with guys, and I get all hot and tingly, and I want to know. But he hurt me … and when I cried and threatened to run, he took my clothes and put them in the bathroom while he showered. I didn't want to be a virgin. Oh, god, I'm not a virgin anymore …" She grabbed the sheet and pulled it up over her face. "Why do I feel ashamed? Why is it so sad and why do I feel so hurt and why did I want to hit him? If it's so good, what did I do wrong?"

By the end of her tirade, tears were running down her cheeks. Jesse couldn't help himself. He pulled the girl into his arms and comforted her.

"It's not that you lost that little bit of skin. It's how you lost it. Is he a friend? Or a boyfriend?"

"Kind of a boyfriend. He goes to junior college in Savannah where I go. I'd talked to him a few times. He said if I came into Savannah on the weekend, and went out with him, he'd drive me home."

"Did he hurt you? You know, force you, or, oh shit, a man needs to let a woman kind of catch up, if you know what I mean."

"He was different. Angry. Bossy. He threw me on the bed and asked me if I wanted to get fucked. He turned me over, pinned my arms down and came at me from behind. That's not love."

"Damn, sweetheart. You sure picked the wrong guy. And no, that's not love. It's not even good sex."

"I don't know what you mean. I don't know anything, and I want to know *everything*. Tell me. *Show* me."

Fuck all.

"You don't want me to do that. There's nothing for us. You must know that. Besides, I'm getting on a plane today. I don't plan to ever come back here."

"But that's perfect. My mama will never find out. I'll know what's right and I won't be afraid to try things with boys 'cause I'll know if they're doing it wrong." She rolled her eyes. "Please?"

Jesse felt his cock swell under his hand. She had perked up now, and her eyes were gleaming with excitement. *It wouldn't be like I was deflowering an innocent, would it? Maybe …*

"I have to get up and pee, and I have to brush my teeth and you should too …"

"I already did," she said, bouncing on the bed.

When he came back from the bathroom, she had shed the shirt and shorts and sat bare naked on the bed with her legs crossed open in that oriental lotus thing with her little pussy exposed. Jesse almost turned around and hid in the bathroom. *She could be under-age. She could be innocent. What have you got to give her, you dumb cowboy?*

"First off," he said, "a man likes to look. You don't show him anything you don't want him to look at. 'Cause he will." He reached over and pushed her knees together. "Second. If a man tries to plunge right into you without any foreplay, it will probably hurt. He has to get you wet."

"How does he do that? I get wet sometimes just watching couples make out—even when I imagine boys touching me."

This one is so ripe. "Well, he might kiss you."

"I like that. I've been kissed."

"Well, honey, sweet kissing ain't anything like sex kissing. It's much more of everything. More times, more places, more penetrating. There's tongues and licking."

"Licking? Why licking?"

"Because the tongue is hot and wet and it can go places, and it's kind of a replacement for the, you know, cock."

Shit. Why am I trying to explain this? "Here I'll show you about kissing." He scooted across the bed until they were close and took her face between his hands. He kissed her gently on the lips several times, moving around to sense the shape and feel of them, then biting her lower lip, a tiny nip. She returned by opening her mouth more, and he put his tongue tentatively in it and started rolling it around hers. He pulled back and went in again, pulling her closer. She was responding all right.

"And then there's the kissing in many places," he said. He made his way down her neck and arm. She was firm and toned and soft all at the same time. *Perfect velvet.* Her breasts were small and tight, and the nipples were standing erect. He took one, hot and sweet, in his mouth.

"Oh, I see," she said, startled a bit. "I see. A kind of shiver runs down to my belly like when my grandpa used to tickle me, and I would get the giggles, but it's not funny anymore."

Maybe not funny, but she was smiling all the same, and he noticed.

"Do it again." She looked at him eagerly. "Do the other one."

He did. Her chest began to rise higher, and her breath quickened. He found his hand on her thigh before he meant to go there. Her hips were pulsing against his leg.

"Now I have to touch you there, so I'll know if this is working. Is that okay?"

"I think so. So far so good."

He wondered fleetingly what kind of asshole messed this piece of honey up so bad. He wanted to punch him, but he forgot entirely as he brushed her clit and she thrust up against his hand. *Back to that later,* he thought. He spread her thighs and ran his fingers down into her pussy. Oh, yes, she was wet. Close to dripping. *Slow down now. Don't mess this girl up again.*

"Okay, that's great," he said. "See how ready you are? That means he can get into you without hurting you. If that asshole didn't get you at least this far, he was stupid. No real man wants a woman that's dry. She should be ready. Wet is ready."

Jesse's cock was throbbing. There was no turning back. But there was one more step.

"Do you know where your clit is?"

"I don't know. I've heard of it. I know it's down there somewhere. I tried to find it, but it's all so sensitive. I can't tell what's what."

"Well, I'm going to help you find it. You just tell me when I hit the spot that's most sensitive, okay?"

"Mmmm …" She moaned as he ran his hand up her inner thigh. He felt his way along the lips and found the vaginal opening and just penetrated it a bit with his fingers. She was slippery and hot, and he could feel the blood pumping around his fingers. He wanted to be inside her so much, he didn't know how much longer he could wait, but he wanted her to have what she wanted. He wanted to erase the memory of this awful night. He wanted her to be able to enjoy a boyfriend or a husband one day, not just satisfy him. He moved slowly, spreading the swollen lips as he went, caressing everything along the way, aiming for that hot little nub of intensity he knew lay waiting for his touch. Finding it, he stroked it gently.

The sound she made was the sound men long most to hear from women. A gasp, an intake of the breath, a cry for mercy and a shriek of joy.

"Now do you know why sex is so wonderful?" he asked, rolling his finger slowly around the throbbing nub. Tears were once again running down her cheeks. He knew the difference between those tears and the ones last night. To make a woman cry with pure pleasure like that! Her body was vibrating, and her mouth was open sucking in air, and her pussy was spasming with need.

"I'm going to come into you now," he said. He spread her legs open and knelt over her. "I'm going to go slow. You tell me if anything hurts."

"Yes. Yes. Sorry, I can't talk. I do want you to."

When the head of his cock touched her vaginal opening, he shuddered and almost lost it. She didn't resist him, and he eased his head in without any problem. Once inside he stopped and asked her if she was okay, was she tender or sore? She moaned something, but it didn't really matter. She was zoned out, and he knew it. He began to pulse slowly, using his hands to gently rock her hips against him. With every thrust, he went deeper until the fullness rose in him. He felt her walls clamp and flush around him with heat and energy. She had cum already. Jesus, how could he have forgotten?

No condom! No condom! The alarm went off in his brain, and he finished on her pubis in almost agonizing pleasure.

They didn't move for a full five minutes. Jesse almost dropped off to sleep but roused himself and looked over at her. Her mouth was open and her eyes big.

"Good Lord," she said. "I don't think even Gloria and Francis have had it like this, or I would have known. I … how can I hide it? I think it's showing all over me. Everybody can see!"

"Just relax," he said. "It'll go away. Just say you had a good time and feel great. Nobody will notice unless you want them to."

She stretched and fell back on the bed smiling. "I want to do that again."

"Well, you can't. I have to get you home before your mother comes back."

❧ ⤙✢⤚ ❧

Jesse drove the rental out of Savannah toward Tybee. The girl chatted most of the way. About her friends. About boys. Thanking him for being so good to her. Asking where he lived and what he did for a living. Jesse made something up. He didn't want her trying to find him later or accusing him of rape one day after she'd had time to think about it. Or worse, some Baptist preacher could get ahold of her and convince her she'd sinned and was going to hell and make her confess who did it.

Her house sat in a wooded lot, small and solitary, typical of the clapboard and shingle homes along the rural coast. Jesse was happy to find there were no neighbors to spy on her morning return.

She went inside and changed into shorts and a tee shirt and brought his clothes back to him. He kissed her goodbye on the mouth, but lightly.

"Come on back any time now, you hear?" She tossed the words over her shoulder as she turned back toward the house, her gangly legs eating up the distance like a young horse.

Jesse recognized the phrase as something her mother might have said to a visiting neighbor. She waved back at him, looking more like a gangly colt than the mare she now was and disappeared into the house. She was on that verge approaching womanhood, and it would take time for her young brain to catch up with her body. He had little doubt she would change a few boys in her life. She was aggressive enough that she would have them eating out of her hand.

The sun was out, and the jet plane was full of happy people for a change—bumping into one another, jostling luggage, rubbing arms. What a night. He realized with a bit of regret that he had never asked her name. It didn't matter now. But there was another name hanging around in Jesse's mind. A woman he planned to look up as soon as he landed in Topeka.

A woman he'd neglected for much too long.

The Hungry Guest

Gina Durden

Shaun stands at his second-floor bedroom window and watches. She's there again, just outside the back door in her robe. She is the wife of a couple who are temporarily staying with him.

A parish vicar can become caught up in so many indulgences of his flock. This couple's home is undergoing repairs from water damage. Their two small children are at the grandmother's house, but there is no room for them all, so Shaun has volunteered his first-floor bedroom. Shaun's wife has already left on a prearranged visit to her parents the previous day, leaving him to attend to the two guests. But such guests are usually no more than a small inconvenience, and this was a gesture with a well-defined conclusion.

They had seemed companionable enough. He a slim pale figure, an anthropologist with a graduate thesis in tow; she a dark, quiet beauty. They had been compliant and grateful to be saved a hotel room for two weeks.

The first night, the wife offered to do clean-up in the kitchen while both Shaun and her husband went off to bed. Shaun went upstairs intending to do just that—sleep—but feeling restless, he paced the floor. His bare feet slapped gently on the hardwood as he shed his clothes onto the bedside chair. Stopping to watch a bright September moon rise from the open window, his gaze landed on her form below in the doorway.

She had stepped out the back door of the house, leaned against the sill and undone her robe. She held it open like broad wings, as if to let a breath of the world inside—and perhaps to let a breath out as well. Her gown underneath was so sheer that he could see the outline of her breasts. It seemed an innocent gesture. Overheated from the kitchen work, she must have come outside to cool off. The event lingered in his mind evoking fantasies, but he tethered them to the night and tried to forget them with the dawn. The following daylight hours he spent in his study working on the week's sermon.

The next night at dinner he notices how she does not look at him. Even when he is speaking, and eye contact would be expected, she only raises her eyes briefly to acknowledge a change of voice, then maintains an intense interest in her plate. Perhaps it is the dominance of her husband who keeps the conversation going well into the evening.

For someone so thin and pale, his voice commands the table. His research is going very well. He expounds far beyond Shaun's interest in the subject, and if he is any judge of response, his wife's as well. Perhaps she has heard it all many times and is inured to the stories.

Again, she repeats her offer to clean the kitchen. Shaun is not about to refuse help. With his wife gone for at least three more weeks, he will have enough work of his own to do. Besides, he knows the woman would feel better about the free board if she can pay him back in some way. The husband, however, is not offering any payment. He seems very much in his own world, settled in on the sofa, smoking an acrid pipe without asking, putting his feet up on the coffee table, leaving his jacket on the back of the kitchen chair.

Now, Shaun stands again watching from his bedroom window. This time, she goes farther out into the yard and leans against the wall where the house makes an angle with the shed. He can see her clearly but in shades of dark and light. The moonlight and her pale figure, her jet-black hair loose and lifting in a night breeze, make him think of witches.

She opens her robe again. This time she undoes the top buttons of her gown as well. He watches, still as a cornered hare, as she brings her hands up to her breasts and cups them. Her thumbs run swiftly over the tips—over the nipples.

He cannot see the hardening nubs, but he thinks he can feel them stiff and hungry under her touch.

His fingers tingle. Her head is thrown back, and her mouth is parted. His lips vibrate and part along with hers, matching the shape of her open mouth.

Her hands are working through the thin fabric, her breasts are covered but so alive that they feel naked to his eyes. Brushing lightly, her fingers rotate around the nipple and areola, then clench and knead the mass of her breasts as if under no control of her own. He can sense her passion from this far away—how much stronger it must be up close.

Like pale birds, her hands flutter down to her waist and over her belly. Her fingers aim down, reaching for the mound that waits there … and they stop. She holds this pose as if hypnotized, her passion stilled by some inner command.

Shaun waits, breathless.

She waits too, halted for minutes in her desire. In a resigned gesture, she hangs her head and brings her hands to her face. He thinks he hears her sobbing. Soon she wipes her eyes and closes her robe. Tying the sash with a quick jerk, she slips inside.

The third evening Shaun has business in town. Having left the guests to fend for themselves, he has eaten a sandwich at the local tavern and returned late. He parks the car quietly and decides to walk in the garden.

The moonlight is so bright he can see every leaf, though each is a shade of gray, not green. He walks through the garden as if through a black and white photograph, then settles on a bench under his father's old mulberry tree and waits for her reappearance. He is not disappointed.

She looks around to see whether there is anyone about. Shaun thinks he is hidden well enough in the shadows, and his clothes are dark. She slips to her place against the wall, undoes her robe and the top buttons of her gown, then once again her hands become her lover. He can see that her face is contorted with both distress and passion. She becomes rougher with herself as if forcing something impossible from her breasts. Her fingers reach down again, brush the mound under her gown and retract. How badly she wants to touch herself and yet she cannot. The wind picks up and blows the robe further apart, lifts the hem of her gown, flattens the fabric against her, defining every curve. She reaches down again, holding longer this time, her hand frozen over the place of her pleasure. She cries out. A sound like a hurt animal.

Her body slumps, her legs spread a bit, and she grasps her mound with a passion, squeezing and mauling it. She begins to slap at her mound repeatedly, wanting to punish it for being there, for being so impossible to ignore. Soon she is sobbing and sliding down against the wall, keening a low and painful sound as her body sags to the ground. Her downward slide has caused the gown to rise, so her thighs are exposed.

Shaun imagines a thick dark bush—thinks he can see it between her legs. He cannot be still. He rushes to her.

"Thea ... Mrs. Callahan ... are you all right? Are you?"

She glances up at him with tear-filled eyes for just a moment before her legs take charge and lift her up to run. He grabs hold of her around the waist and pulls her against him in an iron grip. She starts to cry out, and he puts his hand over her mouth. His mouth is against her ear. She is like an animal caught in a trap, wiggling for release. He is afraid she might try to bite him.

"You can't go inside like this. Be still." He squeezes her tighter to affirm his intent. "Be still. Please."

Her body acknowledges his command, though he is not so sure about her mind. Like a frightened animal, she needs a strong hand and voice.

"If I move my hand, you will not make a sound," his voice insists in her ear.

She calms a bit and nods her head. He lifts his hand.

"Come around here, where we cannot be heard so easily." He takes her hand and walks her to the other side of the shed away from the house and the windows. She follows, resisting the pull of his hand like a child caught stealing, delaying the punishment.

As soon as they are out of earshot, she begins to babble.

"I'm sorry. I'm so sorry. I should not have done that. I'm a good wife. I'm a good mother. I was wrong. I shouldn't have these feelings. You shouldn't be holding me like this—"

He backs up against the shed wall, pulls her to him and places a firm kiss against her moving lips— one hand around the back of her neck, capturing her head and the other around her waist. When she attempts to step back, he wraps one leg around her knees and traps her there until she is still. He continues to kiss her—her mouth, her eyelids, and her cheeks. He covers her face with kisses, so he feels the tears when they start.

Instead of pulling away then, she meets him full force with her mouth, kissing him through the tears streaming down her face. They kiss until they are both satiated with it. Their mouths are tingling and hungry. Their tongues are engaged like freed muscles, and they suck each other with force, pausing only to breathe and finally to rest. Her mouth so wild, she has not forgotten how to kiss, nor forbid herself from it.

He is locked against her body and cannot find a way to let go. He has risen hard inside his trousers to her passion and feels he must not break the spell she is under. It could all end right now. He has to say something to bring her back to him and opens his mouth to speak.

She seems to know this and speaks first.

"What good will it do?" she half-whispers. "There is no future in it."

"Must it have a future?"

"I will only return to the pain I already bear. Wanting this even more, knowing that pleasure has come and gone again."

"You must deal with this creature inside you who wants to hurt yourself for desiring. I saw how you fight with your own body. That cannot go on. You were near hysteria."

"I've tried, God, I've tried. I do fight with myself. And no one wins."

He feels her slipping away from him. Already she is turning her body away toward the house. Out of his reach. He tugs her arm, and she turns her face back to him.

"I will not hurt you," he says. "I can help you."

"Can you?" Her eyes are wide and credulous, but once again the caught animal is there as well, trying to flee.

Maybe, he thinks, *maybe she will let me.*

"You must want to do this," he says. She has to make the decision. "If you come out the door again and stand where I can see you, I will know you say yes. I will be here for you."

Her last glance, a lingering wide-eyed question, leaves him hoping. He waits in the garden for ten minutes so as not to associate his return with hers, then slips in quietly through the basement door and up the back stairs to his bedroom.

The next night she does not come. Nor the one after that. Dinners are somber and filled with prating about trivialities and technicalities. Shaun brings out the wine he usually saves for special occasions, hoping to temper the loquacious husband. While Brian Callahan tips back several glasses, Shaun sips one glass delicately. He notices that Thea is doing the same.

Later that night she comes out again, stands by the wall and opens her robe, but she does not touch herself. Shaun is by her side as fast as he can slip down the stairs and out the basement door. He takes her hand and leads her back inside, not through kitchen door but downstairs and into the basement of the house. The small room is dark, lit only by moonlight.

"This is a very solid house. We won't be heard here."

"I doubt he'll hear much of anything tonight." She smiles.

He kisses her. Standing in the middle of the room, their arms wind around each other like climbing roses. He begins to sense her, running his hands around her waist and then around her buttocks and hips taking in the shape of her, the fullness and firmness, letting her know how much he delights in her body. She begins to respond. He reaches down to her mound and presses his hand against her. She starts back.

"I'm afraid. Shaun," she said. "I don't know if I can do this. I've closed that off for so long …"

"Do you want to? That's the only question you need to answer."

"My mind wants to, and my heart wants to, but my body will not. My father … he was a preacher. He forbade us to touch ourselves in any way. Even when I succeed in placing my own hand there, the sensations go away. My body stiffens. I've tried myself for years. This resistance is what I fight."

"Do you trust me?"

"Yes, I do."

"Do you believe that I will not hurt you no matter what?"

She looks deep into his eyes.

"I do believe that. I'm not sure exactly how or why, but I do."

"Then there are ways we can make it happen. I must dominate your body so you cannot resist."

She looks startled. "Why would you want to dominate me?"

"I don't want to dominate you. I want to release you. Your body is fighting what it wants, and something stronger has to stand up to it."

"Maybe I am not as trusting as I thought ..." Her eyes close slightly, her gaze retreating.

"We will go slow, and you will see. You will agree with each move we make before we do it. How does that sound?"

She studies his dark figure. "Slow sounds good."

"Come I will show you one thing." He leads her to the bed. He has not turned on any lights, and she can barely see what is there, but Shaun knows all the shapes and contours of this room. All the objects in drawers, and behind doors and in locked cabinets. He lays her down slowly on the shadowy bed. He takes one arm and stretches it up over her head. He slips a fur-lined handcuff around her wrist and fastens it snug then takes the other arm and does the same.

"I'm going to stretch your arms over your head. This is so you cannot touch yourself, and you cannot resist my touching you. Do you agree?"

"I don't know." She pulls her cuffed arms back down over her chest. "Leave my clothes on. Don't take them off."

"Okay, if you agree for me to raise your arms, I will not take your clothes off."

"Then I agree."

"So here we go." He lifts each arm over her head and attaches the bonds to the bedposts on each side of the bed. He leans over and kisses her on the mouth, running his hands up the underside of her arms, pushing the robe out of the way as his hands gently caress her pale soft skin.

He begins to kiss further down her body. He kisses her neck and her chest, her breasts and her nipples through the fabric. Then, he unbuttons the top buttons of her gown.

"You promised," she says.

"I'm not taking anything off," he says, smiling slyly and continuing to unbutton. He bares her chest and then both her breasts. They gleam alabaster in the moonlight, round and full. Her areolae are dark and small. The nipples are fleshy and large like those of a nursing mother. He kisses them both and suckles them. She begins to squirm with pleasure, this time smiling.

"This is the pleasure my babies gave me," she said. "I was so turned on nursing. I let myself enjoy that as long as I could. That was when Brian began to lose interest …"

"No talk about him now," Shaun orders. "This is about you." He puts a finger on her lips. She opens her mouth and takes it in, sucking and licking it.

"I want to touch you," she says.

"But you cannot," he replies. "You can do nothing. And you cannot stop me doing." He watches to see if she will respond to his dominance and notes that her breathing becomes faster. She tosses a bit within the limited movement her bonds allow.

"You may want to resist, but that will only defeat us," he declares.

He intends to unbutton the rest of her gown, but the opening only goes to the waist. He reaches into a side table drawer and takes out a pair of scissors. "You are about to have a very unhappy accident with your gown." She grimaces. He cuts the fabric from the hem to the point where the buttons end and folds the thin gown open and away from her body, exposing every inch of her. She has not worn panties. He smiles, convinced that at least this part of her body is here willingly.

"You are much too sly. Perhaps for your own good, sir."

There is an edge to her voice. A reaction he has been waiting for.

"You think you can make me stop, but, you see, I am fighting a battle with your wits, and I will win this one."

She still has her legs clamped tightly together—her only defense now that her hands are bound. Shaun stands, takes one leg in hand, and wraps a third furry cuff around the ankle. He stretches its tether around the bedposts and over to the other ankle, attaching another cuff firmly to the other ankle as well. Her legs are spread wide, and her bush is indeed dark and full.

He pulls the tether tight until her legs are parted as far as the tether will allow. "I don't remember agreeing to that," she states, twisting about with her hips, the only part of her body she can still move.

"Which part of you? The one who wants this to happen, or the one who wants to go back to holding all of that desire inside until it eats you up."

She tries to pull her legs together. He can see the cuffs tightening around her ankles, pulling at the skin. But there will be no tell-tale red marks left there.

"The more you struggle, the more it will hurt."

Her legs are tense, straining against the bonds. He takes one in hand and begins to massage just above the ankle, then slowly circling and squeezing the calf, sliding smoothly up behind the knee and lifting it gently to release the tension. He runs his hands up to her buttocks from behind and back to the knee, then up the inner thigh until he nears her cunt. She struggles, whimpering to be let go. He forces her leg still. She struggles again, and again he forces her still until she lets go. Then he takes up the other leg, working it the same.

"I don't think I like this," she says. "I want to get up now."

"I know you do, but you can't. I know the part of you that wants this, and I will only listen to her."

"You can't do this. I'll scream."

"Your husband may hear."

"I'll scream softly. I'll bite you the next time you get near my mouth."

"I'll gag you. Do you want that?"

She shuts up.

He lifts her knees the little he can and pushes them outward. "You should see the beautiful sight I have here. This magnificent cunt, waiting, longing, hungering for someone to invade it. Will it be me?"

He climbs up onto the bed between her legs, puts his hands on either side of her cunt and pushes outward. "You want to open yourself to me. I know you do. You're afraid, but there's nothing to be afraid of. Only that you will feel again, and you want to do that, don't you?"

"Yes." Barely a whisper.

"Don't you?"

Again. "Yes. yes."

He dips a finger into her already wet pussy, drags it out and holds it up to her face. He rubs the scent under her nose. "Do you see that you are wet already, that your body wants this. Your rigid mind wants to deny yourself such a beautiful gift."

He slides the finger back in her cunt, then out through the lips and onto her clit, dragging the moisture with it. Gently he begins to massage the tip of her now hard clit. She jerks and tries to move away.

"What you could not touch, I can touch for you. Let this part of you wake up again. Let it feel again what it was meant to feel."

"I don't know how," she says, squirming.

"I will touch you. As much as I want. You have no say in this. You are not responsible. I am. And I will do this."

"No," she says, softer this time.

"You can blame me. Tell that voice in your head that it can blame me."

He increases the movement of his finger to larger circles and more insistent pressure.

"You love this. You've been waiting for this for so long, and now it's here. You can relax and let it happen to you. Breathe deep, counting it in and out. Deep breaths, and when you blow out, push the energy down into your cunt, out of your naughty head, and into your clit." He sees her doing it, trying, helping at last. "Oh, yes. You're dripping now. I can see the moisture glisten on your pussy. Your body knows what it wants."

"I do want this," she cries. "I do. I do. I don't even remember how. How do I let go?"

Shaun reaches under the bed and pulls out a short multi-thonged whip.

"You have to forget everything else. Forget who you are. Forget where you are. This will help." He drags the thongs over her mound down into her crotch and back over the mound, teasing with it. Then he stings her across the thigh with it. She cries out. Teasing and slapping the other thigh, just hard enough to take her mind off her tension. Then again on her belly, on both sides, then teasing her breasts with it. Slapping her mound again and again. Slapping and then caressing, again and again.

"Is this what you wanted? To punish yourself? I saw you slapping yourself like this." He hits her again until he knows it stings and he can see small red welts forming. She whimpers softly now with every sting. "How much more will it take for you to give up this fight?"

Tears stream down her cheeks and she inhales and exhales a ragged breath. He drops the thong and buries his mouth into her pussy, licking her clit, running his tongue around it in a passion of motion, sucking at her juices. She is moaning now, and he feels her hips begin to move, her vagina begins to spasm and pulse. He unzips his pants and frees the erection that has been rearing up inside them.

Back to her cunt, he works her clit, and then his fingers are in her, two then three. She is slick and opening for him now, her lips purple with desire and so wet. He feels for her g-spot and makes a moving vise between her clit and her g-spot, working both. She begins to moan under his constant rubbing. More and more he arouses her until he thinks she will never release, but neither will he give up, and then at last she arches her back and shudders and he sees the pulse of her belly and feels the quiver of her legs against his, convulsing with pleasure. He feels the flow like an exhalation of energy around his hand. So much held in. He lets her have the orgasm all for herself and when she is finished—he loses count of the number of spasms—he enters her and feels her shudders rippling around his cock. He comes hard and deep with great spastic gushes.

They don't need the restraints after that. For the next two weeks, they are insatiable with each other, taking advantage of every sleepless night and every absence of her husband, who remains busy with trips to the library and the local scientific guild.

Contrary to moral convention, her husband never suspects. Repairs on the couple's house are finished, and they depart, not to be seen again. Well, except for the occasional liaison later in the village, and once or twice when his wife was away again. Shaun makes certain she can help herself whenever she chooses.

She asks Shaun repeatedly how a parish vicar happens to be set up for domination in his basement. He manages not to answer, becomes evasive and jokes until finally he simply smiles.

Sunday sermons are both a pain and pleasure when she is there with her husband. He learns to rise above the desire, and not to rise below. But when she smiles, something she had rarely done before, and he feels her warm, dry hand gripping his hand after the service, he can hardly contain himself.

Ministering to his flock can be such a pleasure.

If She Loved Him

Amelia Allende

If she loved him, it was only that she loved herself through him.

They met seven years before, standing on the banks of the Truckee River, remarking at how nature surprises—how liquid can feel like stone at just the right angle. The day they met, the sky was indecision gray, low clouds pushing pressure into their lungs, destabilizing blood gasses and stasis. They were friends ever since, growing closer as time went by.

Leo was an architect, and Maya was a sculptor. Used to seeing life framed in rough sketches and the wet, amorphous potential of plaster, they each had the enviable ability to be brought to tears in the face of a beautiful building. They were born and raised on different sides of Reno, Nevada, but felt like they had known each other for a lifetime. They were made of the same clay dust and snowmelt, the same western sensibilities and anxieties. Over the years, they became indispensable to each other, speaking in the intimate shorthand of twins and soulmates and certain one-night stands. They often used incomplete sentences and dropped articles when they shared their stories, but they held on to each other and understood. They called each other brother and sister, and dear friend, and every other name that fit in the spaces left by previous commitments and vows.

"You bring light to my dark places," Leo told Maya, watching the river one early April morning.

"You find me when I lose who I am," Maya said, arm around him, casual and comfortable in his presence.

Their truths cut through the isolation to which they were so accustomed, illuminating what they might have been, had they just been themselves all along. "This is who we are together," they said, trading laughter, secrets, and truth like currency.

They listened like it was a contact sport, leaning forward, heads tilting at the other. Their words joined in knots of syllables and sound, unfiltered syntax tangled in unspoken intent and trusted assurances.

"Just friends," they said, "that's all this can be. That is enough, given our marriages and spouses. That is all this is."

If it was anything, it was a slow seduction by listening. It was an unplanned song of recognition they sang of each other when they forgot they were singing. It was a prayer for forgiveness for sins they had yet to commit, written on reflections in irises and slips of the tongue. It was a train bearing down with a heat and a howl they never saw coming.

"What scares you?" Leo asked Maya one cold May day at the park off Winter Street, while warming his hands on his coffee cup, stretched out near a park bench on his jacket.

"That I don't know what I really think about anything."

Leo rolled to his side and propped himself up on his elbow in the grass, black curls soaking up the January sun. "That's scary?" he asked.

"God, yes," said Maya. "I don't know what I should be afraid of, so I'm afraid of everything. I don't know what I think about a million things, so I have to think about everything." She thought for a moment longer and lowered her eyes. "It's exhausting."

"Where did you lose yourself, girl?"

"It could have been a thousand places," Maya said, pulling her thick wool cap down a little lower over her bangs. "At a 7-Eleven after a hard night of drinking, after the tenth time I heard 'Hurt' by Trent Resner. Who can say? You just know something is missing," she said as she searched his face.

"You aren't missing anything, to me, Maya. You are just as I imagined you would be."

Maya smiled at him and reached out a hand. "The universe feels more benign when I am next to you."

"It's not that scary," Leo said to her. He squeezed her hand back, holding it just a second too long before letting go.

"Aren't you scared of anything though?" Maya asked, noting her hand was hot, slightly pink where he had touched her.

"I'm scared of not being the man I should be," Leo said as he spun his wedding ring on his finger. "I'm scared I am someone deep inside I have never met before, and I just might like him better. I should be better, you know? When I search myself for what I truly want, not what I say I want, it makes me sick, and I just shut it off."

"So, it's okay to be something you are not, rather than find out who you are?" Maya asked. "Doesn't that defeat the purpose?"

"I am better for it and so are you. Trust me," Leo said to her. "I break everything I love, Maya, just ask my wife. She would tell you I have disappointed her a million times, crushed her spirit—just by asking too much. You don't want to get too close to me, no matter what good things you think you see in me."

"Are you saying you love me?"

"Desperately," Leo said. "I didn't mean for this to happen, believe that. It's been what, seven years we have been friends? I thought I had this together, I thought we were good like this, but I want more. I didn't want to say anything, to ruin this."

"Are you serious?" Maya asked as she sat up straighter. He had always been so committed to his marriage, or at least he said he was. His motto was "one life, one wife," as he repeatedly told her.

Leo nodded.

"But I have told you everything. My past, my issues, my broken-everything. I didn't think this would go anywhere, so I said it all. I thought you were safe." She felt betrayed but didn't know why.

Leo pulled his scarf around his neck a little tighter and didn't answer.

"You know what, I don't trust myself in this conversation anymore," Maya said. She gathered her bag abruptly and got up to leave. "You're my best friend, Leo. I am married, for Christ's sake. What the hell do you want from me?"

"Everything, I guess," Leo said as he looked up at her, earnest. "I'm sorry, but just everything."

Maya turned to leave without answering him.

"I'm sorry," Leo yelled after her.

When Maya lay in bed later that night, her husband deep asleep next to her, she was lost in the damning admission, and the hint of consequence Leo left her with. She had been stable—solid—for years. She had been married to the notion that she had enough for as long as she had been married to James. This suddenly seemed silly and sad. Was she even allowed to admit she wanted more at this midpoint of a commitment? Could she have it?

With the lights out, husband wrapped in their blankets and the innocence of sleep, her hands traveled down her stomach, but just there. She thought of Leo lying quietly in his own bed, listening to his own wife breathing, smelling her soap and shampoo, smelling familiar. This excited her, for some reason, though it shouldn't. She tried to remember when she last touched herself out of need, want, anything, and couldn't remember. She felt tears push against her lids, the sting of salt, and pushed her hand against her middle. She imagined Leo's hands on her, there, but went no further. Holding herself together was work enough. Wanting, after not wanting, was like starting to breathe with clotted lungs—dangerous but necessary.

She didn't want anything from Leo until he wanted her, and she hated him for this. If she was on fire, she should have started it herself, goddammit. She shouldn't be that quick to turn, to fall, and it made her feel angry and weak and excited all at once. Her husband rolled over to face the wall, tugged the blanket away from her with the weight of him, and her hands traveled down a few inches more. They reached the band of her pajamas, and her entire world view began to slide into her periphery, like the boundaries of her marriage, into that dark grey space between right and wrong, need and want, guilt and absolution.

She thought about Leo over the years of their friendship, all his questions, his laugh, the way he tilted his head so only one errant curl dropped below his brow. She smelled the sweat under his armpits, all those pheromones and hard work— what made him a man. She heard, in her mind, the way her own voice dropped an octave when she talked to him, like she had been smoking, or sleeping, for a very long time. She never noticed this before, but now it seemed obvious, stitched in time over the years and so many light touches on cotton cuffs and suited shoulders and smalls of the back. She thought of love and loss, and "I do," and

"I'm sorry," and all the hours that ached in between. She closed her eyes.

She continued to see Leo every week for coffee on Tuesday afternoons and lunch on Fridays, their usual pattern. She tried to maintain defensible space between their friendship, and whatever was born of his admission to her and her own response, but she was losing ground. For an hour, maybe two, after she left him—she thanked God she didn't drink any more when she might have done something stupid.

One Tuesday in August as she said goodbye at the coffee shop off 9th Street, she thought he was going to lean in and kiss her. She smelled the hazelnut on his breath, they were that close. They pulled apart at the last moment.

She drove home, threw her keys on the table by the door and grabbed gloves, buckets and bleach. She stripped down to her panties and tank top and cleaned the house like a galley slave, on hands and knees and elbows and tile, bruising bones, scrubbing him off her, holding on.

When Maya thought of her husband James, she thought of him like a long-lost friend—someone she loved once but hadn't seen for years. James gave her the same 1950's kiss on the way out each morning after patting her behind. The last time she fell apart when her mother got sick, he watched her cry without leaving his seat at the dinner table. He pushed his chicken and potatoes around the plate and asked careless questions where he thought he should. He acted like he was trying. That's what

Maya thought. He sat there, silent, and watched her contract as his indifference expanded. She thought about the last time they had sex. She thought of how she turned away after, hungry for air and release from empty communion with an irrelevant god. He had rolled off her, satisfied, and she had shut her eyes against the aftermath of sex in a body that didn't feel like her own anymore.

She couldn't identify her voice in this marriage after all these years, as if the marriage had started speaking about her in the third person while she was still in the room. She could see James and herself as they were years ago, a black and white silent film playing on a loop, dancing on their wedding day, sitting on the beach with tighter bodies and a stronger connection, crossing the threshold of their first home. But that was a decade ago.

She considered investing again in the relationship, pondered what it would take for a few long minutes, then remembered she needed to water the plants. She was now a caricature of herself, she thought, as she carefully cleaned the leaves of her Philodendron and pondered its welfare. She was a woman who mourned a marriage rotting on the vine yet put more time into her greenery than her man.

Thank God she didn't have cats.

Her unraveling happened so slowly she didn't think to jump. She warmed up in Leo's open face and open-ended questions, deaf to the slow ticks on the dial, as she heated from the inside in increments. She stepped further into him and away from James over coffee, long lunches and walks back to the office by the river.

Every conversation, every phone call was freighted with the unsaid things that were in the room with them. She began to like the attention Leo gave her, crave it even. She trusted his view of the world and his perspective on her. She started to think he might be the something she needed, and she began to want more.

In his adoration and invitation, she warmed and bubbled until she began to smell smoke everywhere, all the time. She found smudges of ash on the bedsheets when she slept and little, heated footprints on the tile in the bathroom that glowed radioactive. There were charred holes in her clothes where her desire had burned through, venting her. She vigilantly patched them with bits from the bag full of her grandmother's scarves she had saved for a rainy day and began to pray for actual rain. She started wearing less and less, and she roamed the house after work in boy shorts and a camisole, sometimes just the shorts as she hunted for her old life in the corners and the cabinets.

She was sweating all the time, burning through boxes of deodorant and powder and panty liners. She stopped putting on cocoa butter after a shower because it trapped the heat until she smelled like baking brownies, and the neighborhood dogs started following her on her walks around the block.

Waking at night in blooming orgasms of surprise, and thanked God for small favors like waking dreams and the memory foam mattress that soaked up the trembling and kept her secrets. Her plants started wilting one after the other, not made for the longing that filled her house with tropical heat. She watched them die and promised herself she would remember to water the next day and the next, but she never did.

Maya read with ice on her forehead in bed at night, and it melted against her face, big fat drops making craters on the paper, pooling on her eyelashes and lips. "It must be menopause," Maya told her husband, fanning herself with her hand.

"My mother ran away to Phoenix when she went through menopause," James said. "You aren't planning to bolt, are you?"

"You have nothing to worry about. Phoenix is too hot. Now Alaska, Alaska sounds heavenly."

She and Leo continued to see each other over the coming months, dancing around where their conversations were leading them.

"I know I shouldn't, but I want more of this. Why can't we have more of this? You make me so happy," Leo told Maya one day over lunch at Sabrina's in September. He leaned in, taking up space, penetrating whatever distance they had left to cross before they found each other. She inhaled deeply as he moved into her. Her head filled with the basil from the kitchen, the sage blowing through the open door, and his sweat. She felt fertile and alive, like she was rooting where she sat, like she might open and bloom right there in front of him.

"That's the thing about personal happiness. It's overrated. We have obligations, like husbands and wives and houses and all those future children you want," she said, trying to sound surer than she was.

"You say that," Leo said. "But I know you want this. I make you happy, too."

"You make me a lot of things. It's that listening you do that is so intimate and dangerous," Maya told him.

"I hear you, Maya. I see you." Leo said.

Maya pulled back. "Don't do that. Please. We have no choice. We need to stay like this, in that grey area between what might be and what can't survive this."

"A grey area is not a destination," Leo said to her. "It's a waypoint to either going back or moving forward. You can't have all this from me and keep me here, in your indecision. You might not be able to marry me, but you can have me. That means something, doesn't it?"

"I can't have any *more* and stay who I am. No matter what you do for me."

She was scared of wanting more than her life could hold, and even more afraid of being asked for more than she had to give. She was stuck in the middle of desire without resolution, where all her choices met to consider what had been and what could be. She kept her desire at bay by reading poems by angry women and listening to music so full of longing that it made her fingertips bleed, leaving marks on the countertops and refrigerator handles when she made dinner each night.

She was buying time.

She was sorting herself out.

"I think you are dying," James said one day, seeing the crime scene in the kitchen.

"No, that is definitely not death. It's just change."

"I hope I still recognize you when you are finished with all this changing," he said.

You couldn't pick me out of a lineup, she thought to herself, as she bandaged her fingers in gauze and tape and gathered up the towels. "Whenever you see me, it will be the first time," she said, not realizing she had spoken aloud.

"What is that supposed to mean?"

She didn't answer.

"What does that mean, Maya?" He said a little louder.

"I can't hear you, I'm in the laundry room."

As she started the towels in the washer, she thought of Leo. Leo, who gave her arthritis in her heart and fingers and toes, who stole her peace by recognizing how much she was missing before she realized she had lost anything at all.

⊱──◈──⊰

"I miss you," Leo said to her on the phone one late night in October, after a few weeks of the silent treatment from Maya. "I know you are trying to figure this out, but I miss you."

"I miss you, too."

"Send me a picture? Please."

"Of what?" Maya asked.

"Of something real."

Maya lowered the blankets, lifted up her shirt, and turned her necklace around backward so its recognizable charms hung off her back. She held a breast in one hand, phone in the other. She made sure her face was not visible. She hit send, and freedom was born in the form of a headless selfie, making its way over live wires, a still life confession.

"Jesus," Leo said. "Send me another. Your husband is out of town, this is the only time you can do this."

"No."

"Send me another," Leo said, and Maya sent the stomach she had been running her hands over, one finger hooked on the waistband of her panties at the top of the frame.

"God, I want you."

"I know," Maya said, as she tried to stop the milk coming from her breasts and the blood from her fingers. She gave up and started mixing them together like paint, covering her flesh until the entirety of her smelled like earth and woman, truth and consequences. She hung up the phone and put it on silent.

Her body betrayed her regularly after this, spilling milk and minerals, bursting into flames that scorched the soles of her feet and the palms of her hands. She couldn't understand it. She didn't want a life with Leo. She knew better than to wish for that. She just needed him to make her burn more for a minute and then put her out. She wanted more passion, more anger, more honesty, more pain, more forbidden, more messiness, more longing, and God, please, more trembling. She wanted it all until she was wrung out and content in her own life again until she was as cold as charcoal and just as tough.

She thought if he could wear her longing out with all that desire, Leo might be able to crush Maya into a smiling wife again. If he could take her unsaid desires and make them things she heard outside her body, it might right-size Maya into the life she had created with James. It might make her remember to water the plants again.

"Put your hands on your chest baby girl," Leo told her on a call. "Do you feel me there?"

Maya examined the skin covering her ribs and above her breasts. Yes, there, in muted red was Leo's heat signal to her. Her hand was red in the light, with translucent veins visible against the glow. Maya saw under her palm her own truth, long-protected and suffocated, straining against her, a hostage coming breach. Wild and unbound, her words tumbled into the phone in bed next to her, desire and resignation giving life to what felt like the bastard child of rage and longing. Maya's words slid out now, fast and slippery, the breaking water of a foregone conclusion.

"I want this, I want this, I want this," she said, pushing her fingers inside herself, warm and imperative. She said her own name aloud like a confession, thinking she was giving herself to him, not realizing she was taking herself back.

"To name is to make real," she said to him, tired and spent. "You call me into my own body when you call my name. You know what I need. You say what I need to hear."

"You just called yourself by your own name, Maya," Leo said to her with disdain in his voice. "You didn't say mine. You got yourself off and said your own goddamn name."

Maya looked up to the clock and marked the hour she would cut him loose. Her breath caught with the realization that she felt only herself in that moment and knew she had had enough.

She should have thanked Leo for pulling and twisting this out of her, this pulse between her ribs and legs, this name for feeling again but not needing, but she didn't. She should have told him she appreciated his effort to free her with his claiming, but she wouldn't. He wouldn't understand, and would just interpret it as love returned, and that would never be it. She had found a new faith in desire that shouldn't be allowed to flourish, but did, in a body that called up blood to her skin without fear because it could. She remembered she used to always want more, and that she once again might imagine as much.

"I am not your therapist," Leo said. "You can't just have me by the hour."

Maya paused for a moment and hung up the phone.

Like a gift from a foreign dignity, she was in receipt of all of this, and that was all she would officially say about it. She didn't want to do the math of what it meant to want something she couldn't have and find out she already had what she needed inside her. She has been a thief in this relationship, acting like this thing meant the same thing to both of them, but she would get away with it. Because if Maya ever loved Leo, it was only that she loved herself through him—if she loved him at all.

Imagine

Patrick Bruskiewich

The train gave a small jerk, then another and I closed my eyes to try to imagine how we were slowly starting to move. I had the coach car all to myself. I was in the second row of seats on the starboard side. The overhead lights were off, and I had turned the small, bright overhead spotlight above my seat off so that I could clearly see out the window. The air had that smell only a train could have, of diesel and other indistinguishable odors. It was also at that edge between warmth and coolness, for it was early November and fall was in the air. In short order, the air in the car would turn toasty warm.

It was late on a Saturday night, around 2230, and I was on the red-eye Amtrak train from New York on my way to Boston. We would arrive around five a.m. I traveled quite a lot around the States from one hospital to another, selling medical equipment. This week I had been in to visit a client at Memorial Sloan Kettering in New York.

It had been a productive meeting, and I was very happy with the results. We would soon be signing a rather large and complicated multimillion contract. I had the letter of intent burning a hole in my jacket pocket. I was now off to visit some potential clients at Harvard.

While the weekdays were entirely for business, the weekends were entirely my own. I had spent this particular slow and sleepy Saturday morning enjoying the Greek and Roman collection at the Metropolitan Museum. Then it was time to check out of my hotel, before checking my luggage in at the train station and treating myself to a late lunch at the Russian Tea House. The caviar was superb, as was the fresh pumpernickel bread and homemade butter. The bill was $345, but I convinced myself that was fine—it was a once in a lifetime experience, and I could not imagine any other occasion that would see me treat myself in such a czarist fashion. I knew I had earned it.

It may seem strange, but after the Russian Tea House, I had taken a light supper at a Japanese restaurant not too far from the train station before drifting around a bit window shopping and then hanging out at an upscale bookstore. I took a stack of books to my table as I sat and enjoyed a cup of black coffee.

The table I sat at was a reflection of my life. It was small, round, and had one empty chair. There were no sharp edges in my life, and while I was married, I was very much alone because my wife was into the whole marriage thing for herself and no one else. That left me, the other half, empty-hearted. It was a measure of things that I was happier when I was away from her on a business trip doing what I enjoyed than when I was at home doing nothing of substance.

It really wasn't much of a home. Everything in it glorified my wife right down to her growing collection of expensive dinner place settings and Dalton porcelain. "I will shop 'till I drop," was her mentality, and she spent more than I made. It was like throwing more wood onto an out of control conflagration. I had told her that things had to change or I would keel over one day with a heart attack, but all she could say was, "don't worry dear, we have life insurance." To put things into context, my aged parents called our place the cuckoo's nest … it wasn't mine.

It took me eight long years of melancholic married life for me to realize that everyone has a right to be happy and that no one has a right to steal away one's happiness, least of all the other half of married life. I had begun to imagine a better life but did not know how I would find it.

I was also no longer in a hurry to travel about. I wanted to enjoy every moment of my travel, and imagine a second, happier and secret life, away from the cuckoo and her nest. Flying fast hither and thither was no longer a pleasure to me, and so I thought on this trip from New York to Boston to savor the moment.

I also felt it would be nice to try something new. Train rides were beginning to be a passion for me. Sure, they were slower than plane flights, and a bit more expensive, but they were much better for the body and soul. Besides, I felt happier traveling this way, and I met so many interesting people on my rail travels.

On this particular evening, for the first time in many years, I was happy. Perhaps it was because of how I felt when I sat wondering of the lives of the artists who had carved the Greek sculptures now at the Met. Or maybe it was because I wondered about the man who had made me my caviar somewhere halfway around the world, or perhaps it was the aged sushi chef at that busy restaurant who took such great pains to make each plate a work of art. Maybe it was the gothic barista at the bookstore who had made my coffee, the thousandth cup of her day, or maybe it was thinking how the man on the train got on with his life given its tedium and nocturnal disruption? There was a tingle in me that was hard to explain, let alone understand.

I could feel the shudder of the train gather speed, an anticipation of the adventure ahead. I had never before taken this particular train ride. I had taken the Amtrak between New York and Washington, DC. Before when I had gone from New York to Boston on business, I had flown. This trip, it was time for both a change and an escapade.

We had moved for perhaps a minute when the door at the front of the car swung open hesitantly. I opened my eyes, and there appeared a woman in her early twenties, in a bit of disarray. I could imagine her running frantically to catch this train, the last of the day back to Boston. She and her things tumbled into the seats on the front row opposite to me, and she caught her breath. I don't think she saw me. Perhaps she imagined that the car was completely empty, and she had the whole place to herself.

She let out a sigh, then cleared her throat. Then sighed a second time as she sat wistfully.

I wondered what she was thinking as I studied her in the dim light of the passageway at the front of the coach car. She dressed simply. She wore a thick red sweater, a pale blue pair of jeans and a simple pair of white espadrille running shoes. She carried a small purse, a knapsack and what looked like an artist's sketchbook.

It was her sketchbook and her sweater that gave her away. I realized that I had seen her earlier that day in the Greek and Roman collection sitting on a bench drawing studiously in her sketchbook. I hadn't thought anything about her when I had walked by her at the Met. She had been sketching the *Standing Youth*, or *Kritios Boy*, of the 5th century BC Greek sculptures. But here on the train, it was different. She suddenly became a person of interest for me, if not for the simple reason we would be sharing the journey together, then because of her sketchbook.

Even the books I sat and looked at when I drank my coffee at the bookshop were art books. My visits to the public and private art galleries up and down the Northeast had fanned a long dormant flame in my heart for art. It was not just a business visit to Harvard that was taking me from New York to Boston—it was a chance for a pleasurable visit to the Boston Art Gallery as well. It would be my first visit to the Boston Art Gallery.

She stood up and kneeled on her seat looking back into the coach car. It was then that she suddenly saw me. I smiled, said hello and asked her how her day at the Metropolitan Museum had gone. She was surprised to both see me and to hear me ask such a question.

I turned on my overhead light so that I did not remain a shadow in the dark. "I was at the Met this morning and saw you at the Greek and Roman exhibit sketching. Are you an artist?" I asked her hoping this would defuse the awkwardness of the moment.

She shook her head. "Not really, I am taking an art history course."

"You must be going to university?" I asked.

"I am a student at one of the prep colleges in Boston. And you?"

"I am on my way to Harvard for a few days."

"You a prof?" There was an edge to her question.

"No ... I sell medical equipment."

"Oh ..." You could almost feel the tension in her melt away.

"You don't like academics, do you?"

"No ... both my parents are academics. And all their friends too."

"At Harvard?" I don't know why I asked her this, but it hit its mark.

"Yup, and they drive me crazy! My parents and all their friends too."

"I can only imagine. Academics drive me bonkers too. I enjoy being with real-life people more."

She giggled.

I smiled.

We had broken the ice.

I offered her my hand. "My name is Patrick."

"I am Lydia." She reached over and shook my hand.

"Let me guess …"

"Guess what?"

"You took the early train to New York so that you could go to sketch at the Met, and now you are scurrying home before anyone notices?"

She giggled a second time. "You're good, but not perfect."

"No one is perfect, that I can tell you."

"You can—"

"From personal experience?"

"The hard way?" She was playing with me.

I nodded.

"You married?"

"Not really."

"I thought that question had only two answers, yes or no?"

"There is also being unhappily married."

"The hard way?"

I nodded. "How did your sketches turn out?"

"Do you want to see them?"

"Yes please." She snatched up her sketchbook and sat down, turned on her overhead light, then motioned for me to join her and sit next to her. I got up and crossed the aisle.

"Is the train always so empty?" I asked her.

"There are people in the other coaches," she said.

"I chose this coach because it was empty," I confessed to her.

"You must be like me. I like quiet places. I don't like being around noisy people."

I smiled as she said this. She had her sketchbook on her lap. I noticed a large art textbook in her knapsack. Lydia opened her large sketchbook. It was a new book, and she had filled the first few pages with her sketches. They were proficient, but I immediately noticed something missing.

"You sketched everything about the sculptures except that what makes them male." As I said this she blushed.

"I can't ..."

"Can't what?

"I can't bring myself to draw their naughty bits."

I laughed.

"What's so funny?"

"Naughty bits! I haven't heard that since I was at Catholic middle school."

"You're Catholic too!" Lydia exclaimed.

I nodded. "But that has never prevented me from drawing the naughty bits of girls."

"We don't have naughty bits." She was earnest as she said this.

"Come on. Girls don't have naughty bits too?" I leaned away as she said this.

"No, we don't!" I wondered if she was just flirting with me.

"May I?" I pointed to her art book. She nodded and handed me her book. I opened it and searched for the painting I was looking for—Botticelli's *The Birth of Venus*.

"See? Women have breasts, a clitoris, and a vagina—for a boy, those are naughty bits." She blushed even more but remained silent. "Us boys have …" I stopped and looked at her, wondering why she did not finish my sentence. I opened the textbook to a new section and turned the pages until I found one of the sculptures in her textbook that she had sketched earlier at the Met. I set the book onto her lap. "And what do boys have?"

She all but stuttered as she tried to say the p-word.

So, I said it for her. "A penis. Boys have a penis."

"Penis," she repeated, in a nervous giggle.

"You have never said that word before, have you?" I could feel the nervous warmth of her as she shook her head. "Do you want me to stop?" She shook her head slowly a second time.

"What else do boys have in the way of naughty bits?" She shrugged her shoulders, so I continued. "We have testicles and a scrotum, marbles in a marble sac. Have you not had a boyfriend?"

Her lips pouted as she said, "No. My parents won't let me."

I could sympathize with her. "When I was in school my parents did not let me out of their sight. Not that they didn't trust me … but they are very Catholic."

"So are mine."

"So … repeat after me. Penis."

"Penis …"

"Testicles …"

"Testicles." She managed to merge the words test and icicles in a fashion I had never heard before.

"Scrotum …"

"Sco-thumb."

Close enough, I thought. "Did you study biology in high school?" I asked.

"No, I took chemistry and physics but not biology." I could tell that Lydia was disappointed. "My parents are not science types."

"Oh, what do they do?"

"My mother is an English professor, and my father teaches law."

"And you are the only child, aren't you?"

"How did you know?" Lydia was genuinely surprised.

"It seems rather obvious. Two profs for parents. You also strike me as a lonely type. If you are an only child, then you are by nature a lonely type."

She went silent.

I went back to admiring her drawings. "Your sketches are very well done. What are they for?"

"I am taking an art history course about ancient Greek and Roman sculpture."

"Does it embarrass you that most of the sculptures are naked males?"

"When I decided to take the course, I didn't know that most ancient Greek and Roman sculptures were of naked men."

"Did you think they were about naked women?"

She shook her head. "I didn't think any of the sculptures were naked."

"Now you know. Are you disappointed?"

"No, not really. It just takes some getting used to. Can I ask you something?"

I turned to her and looked into her eyes. Her irises were fully opened. "Sure, you can ask me anything you want."

"Are you like this?" She was pointing down at a picture of the *Kritios Boy.*

"Well ..." I looked down at the picture then looked up at Lydia and said playfully, "Yes and no."

"In what way yes?"

"I have the naughty bits."

"In what way no?" She looked at me puzzled.

"Well, he is a boy. Boys and men are different."

"In what way?"

"I could use words to try to describe the difference, or I can let you find out for yourself."

"What!"

"Let us turn off the light, and I will let you find out for yourself."

Lydia hesitated, looked down at my lap as she decided. Then she reached up and turned off her overhead light. We were now both alight in the glow of the passageway.

I reached down and unbuckled my belt and unbuttoned the top of my pants. Then I slowly unzipped my pants. I whispered to Lydia, "Be gentle, no pinching."

I looked at her face as she peered down at my lap. Her right hand was cold and hesitant. Lydia was obviously very nervous. She slowly reached in under the elastic band of my briefs. When she had felt the first of me, she stopped, and her fingers slowly traced a circle. This tickled me. The circle grew in radius until it encompassed the tip of me.

Then with a finger, she followed the one crease that went from tip to the base.

She was very careful and meticulous with her touch. Lydia was not in a hurry to experience the wholeness of me. Next, she let her hand glide past the tip of me until she felt the shaft of my penis.

"You are so soft," she whispered. "And so warm."

I whispered back, "That is something boys and girls share, softness and warmth."

I opened my legs further to invite her to continue her exploration, and she did, advancing slowly down to my scrotum. When she held my testicles in her hand, she gulped in a long amorous sigh.

Lydia leaned forward and whispered into my ear, "May I see?"

I was about to say yes, but his timing was so wrong. The door to the back of the coach started to rattle and open. I knew that only the conductor would be moving up the train at this point in the voyage. Lydia pulled her hand out from my briefs, and I quickly gathered myself up, and zipped and buttoned and belted myself just in time.

When the conductor found us, we were both quietly admiring the sketches in Lydia's sketchbook. We hadn't had time to turn the overhead light back on, so the conductor did it for us.

"Everything in order?" the conductor queried. We both nodded but did not say a word.

I imagine the conductor has seen his fair share of intimate moments on the train. I imagine the conductor probably suspected we were sharing such a moment. He let us be and proceeded to the next carriage, but not before informing us he would be passing back this way in ten minutes. It was at that moment that I felt a twinge of embarrassment. I could feel my feet get cold.

I turned to look into Lydia's face. It shone in the pale light of the passageway.

What she said surprised me. "Yes, there is a big difference." She emphasized the word big. I smiled as she did this. "Can I?"

"Maybe after the conductor has come back through." It made sense, but she was disappointed nonetheless.

I pointed to her sketchbook. "Why don't you sketch the sculpture's naughty bits?" She searched into her knapsack for her pencils and was avidly sketching when the conductor came through when he said he would. Lydia sketched for nearly an hour before she set down her pencil. Her new sketches were from several angles and were more prominent than those of the *Kritios Boy*.

When she set down her pencil, I asked whether she would like to grab something from the cafeteria car. She nodded, and I grabbed my briefcase, and she her knapsack and things, and we both walked to the rear of the train. I walked behind her noticing the sway of her hips and the fact she had very athletic legs.

The cafeteria car was three coach cars back. The two coach cars had a smattering of people. There were a handful of people in the cafeteria car. We sat, and the porter immediately came to ask us for our order.

"It is good you came just now. It is the last order."

We both ordered some herbal tea. The porter poured a new bowl of peanuts for us, and we chatted a bit.

"Thank you," she said.

"You're welcome. All in the name of art."

"And other things!" She had a big smile on her face as she said that.

Our teas arrived, and we lifted and clinked our cups. "To other things," I said.

"Can I ask you something?" Lydia had a timid look on her face.

I nodded.

She leaned over and asked quietly, "I would like to sketch you."

"I know you would, and the answer is yes." I hesitated. "Can I ask you something too?"

"I know what you will ask … and the answer is yes. It seems only fair." Lydia paused and then said, "There is only one thing …"

"And what's that?" I whispered.

"I am a virgin and a Catholic."

"I am a Catholic but not a virgin," I responded.

"Please don't ask me to …" She blushed and looked down at her shoes.

I placed my hand on hers and said, "If you don't want me to. When are you expected back at your college?" I asked her.

"By my first class on Monday," she answered.

"Will you take me to the Boston Art Gallery Sunday afternoon?"

She nodded.

"Do you want to stay with me today?" Lydia smiled and nodded, then she took my hand in hers and held tight as we both enjoyed our midnight tisane.

I looked at her, and the swaying of the train echoed the bliss of the moment.

Stage Hand

Grüdier

She held the outfit aloft after a final stitch. Though little more than glittered straps, it was captivating. The costume did appear wide enough to cover appropriate places and suited the act she described to us earlier.

The show premiered the next evening, scheduled at a popular local venue I was familiar with both as a performer and a guest. Our friend described her routine as a fusion of burlesque and acrobatics on an aerial apparatus she also designed.

Studying her creation, Rüdi appeared transfixed, and I am sure he wanted to ask her to try it on. We were all lounging half-naked anyway. She would have said okay and done so, but he wouldn't have been serious. She had been a good friend for a long time, and now our roommate, but had not lived with us long enough to recognize his innuendos.

She faced me and offered, "I have a pass for the show tomorrow evening if you want to go, though only one." She did know Rüdi well enough to know he is less than a fan of burlesque.

We have both heard him say, and more than once, "Sexualizing nakedness restricts opportunity. The practice relates to the shame and guilt many experience in their sensual expression."

"It kills you when performers end their show after they remove most of their clothes," I said, laughing.

"Nudity portrayed as naughty is annoying," Rüdi corrected. "They often run off and feign embarrassment. They are still wearing three pieces of clothing, two pasties, and a thong."

"Three garments is a lot of clothes," I said with my usual salt of sarcasm.

"Yeah, no one counts shoes," Rüdi said. "Cosette, do you recall reading Gibran?"

"I remember," I remembered. "Your clothes conceal much of your beauty."

"My costume is only one piece," said our friend. "It doesn't conceal much."

The design was bold—the lack of coverage daring, even for a burlesque dancer.

"I couldn't go if I wanted to," Rüdi insisted.

She stuck out her bottom lip in a faux pout so he added, "I would go, but a stack of work waits, and I am not doing it this evening." He gestured toward a disarray of a pile of papers. "Instead, I am hanging out with you two."

Rüdi is not an author, being far too busy with other's writing. Fast and effective, he edits for the pseudonyms of an older, fictional, alternate universe version of himself.

I thanked our friend for the pass.

The next evening, I left Rüdi to attend the show alone, arriving early as usual as I like to watch people arrive. Seated at the restaurant bar, open before the theater, I ordered a bottle of French champagne. The bartender poured a glass and promised to have the rest delivered to my table.

My server would likely be Cat, and we exchanged nods and knowing glances as I entered.

She is an elegant faerie creature who reminds me of Persephone. She is beautiful, thoughtful, determined, and trapped. Trapped in an underground burlesque venue for at least half her life, like Persephone, confined to the underworld for six months each year.

The netherworld is not an evil place, in my understanding. It is not a dungeon or a prison, rather a place where energies congregate after the demise of their last physical form, like bees concentrate in hives and people gather in cities.

It must have been a great job, working in a performance hall, though I imagined Cat preferred to be free, running through forest fields and grassy meadows, stripping off her clothes in the warm sun and light wind. She would end up at least as naked as the performers, and I considered the contrast.

Burlesque dancers performing for fans compared with a bare-skinned, lone young woman naked in a meadow. Her long hair would float over and around her like a halo, a dancing tsaheylu with the leaves of the trees and the grasses in the breeze.

I thought more of Gibran's words, "Would that you could meet the sun and the wind with more of your skin and less of your raiment."

Perhaps she is more inhibited than that, I do not know her all that well. If so, it may derive from escalating puritanical morals of a current generation. It would not come from her essential character.

"For the breath of life is in the sunlight and the hand of life is in the wind."

Gibran's words are always powerful and often instructive, his writings suggest the life force is the source of health, of wholeness. The power of life animates dead matter, it awakens and feeds conscious awareness. According to Gibran, that same energy is also a potent healing element.

In the Greek language the word for life, the Chinese chi, is eros. Erotic energy is that which arouses, excites, and is essential to the process of procreation. Nudity supports and enhances the life force, that eros. Erotic energy supports and enhances arousal and orgasm as well. Not just in the sexual realms, but in the peaceful bliss and overwhelming joys of life.

Rüdi may be right, nudity is too important to be relegated to the sexual realms, especially in the current austerity of the fragile generation. Pretending that bare skin is naughty, that sex is naughty, is a restriction of opportunities for health and longevity—ecstasy and delight.

The legends of the gods, such as Persephone, were far more than myths. At least from the objective "fair witness" perspective I held. The legends could be histories and accounts of great deeds of remarkable humans. Or they could be tales of supernatural beings living on Earth in alternate dimensions and along alternate timelines.

I fantasized and considered Cat might even be Persephone, hiding among us or unaware of her true nature. Would a sort of physical arousal awaken the memories surely stored in some invisible and inaudible energetic plasma within or surrounding her? Someone might call this an aura, but I perceived it more as energy fields.

Persephone sealed her fate in the underworld when tricked by her captor Hades, she ate six pomegranate seeds. Cat worked here serving clients because, like the goddess, she must eat. Her destiny may be tangled up with this venue and the burlesque shows performed there.

My mind stopped wandering, and I noticed people were slow to arrive. I wandered downstairs into the underground theater and noticed the merchandise table and a couple setting up smiled at me. I drifted deeper when Cat walked up beside me with the ice bucket under an arm and asked, "May I show you to your table?"

"Yes," I replied, not wanting to sit down yet, but excited to follow Cat to the front of the space. It was a crush. She was sensual, vibrant, honest, and earthy. I knew the location of the table but was happy she was my guide. The table was close to a corner stairway to the stage with an aisle for dancing during live concerts.

She led me through the maze of seating, and it gave me an opportunity to inspect her clothing. She wore an above-the-knee black skirt over smooth, bare legs, and a red button-down shirt. Her top, buttoned low, hinting she may not be wearing a bra. A gold necklace hung around her neck set with a clear quartz crystal. Her shoes appeared comfortable, black patent leather showing the cleavage of her toes. I wondered if she wore panties.

We were wearing similar colors, red, black, and gold on our light skin—like the customary attire at the Moulin Rouge in Paris. Moulin Rouge, like the Lido, is a less than inhibited venue. The artists are often topless, always stunning, talented, and dancing live in magnificent venues.

I was in a short, red cotton dress with gold chains holding it over my shoulders and strappy black leather, crystal glitter heels. A black ribbon held my hair in place off my neck. A red lacy silk bow backed thong completed my outfit. I realized the two pieces of clothing I had on were one less than a burlesque dancer's three.

Red is the color of passion, red is sexy. Red is fresh blood, rubies, roses, and pomegranates. A color at the end of the visible spectrum blending into a color humans cannot see—infrared.

Pomegranates epitomize the hue. Blood-red, the color of danger and far more. Blood-red is a texture, a translucency, a sound like ooze, scents of copper and rust.

Translucent like the oily tint of alizarin crimson, the red in stained glass windows, the near-transparent seeds of the pomegranate. Like sunlight through a ruby crystal, almost see-through, but not quite. Red like the theater's curtains that were, for some reason, not descended all the way. The time may have been earlier than I thought, as preparations for the show were still going on.

We approached the table and I saw a pair of feet walking underneath the curtain. Bare feet. I recognized Marcus, the light man. I know him well as he and I worked together rigging aerial apparatus for two prior shows. His art is light, lighting sets, acts, and actors. For some reason he preferred to work barefoot.

The familiar feet approached as Cat asked if I wanted a refill. She twisted the bottle deeper into the ice with one hand, gesturing toward my empty glass with the other. Before I answered, the side of the drape swung open and Marcus exclaimed, "Cosette! Wonderful to see you." Then he addressed the server, "Cat, I know this is a lot to ask, can you help me for a few minutes?"

She wavered, waiting for my signal to pour champagne but glanced at him, then back at me. I answered for her, "She looks busy Marcus, and I would love to help you."

"Amazing, Cosette, thank you." He waved me up the steps as I set down my empty glass, smiled at Cat, and excused myself to follow him.

"You sure look like you dressed for a burlesque show," Marcus said, watching me as I climbed the stairs. I could see him scanning my body before he hurried ahead to the lighting control panel.

His notice of my clothing was a new thing, more personal. I began to think he might have more than a professional interest in me. I was, of course, attracted to him, to his artistic nature, his casual competence and love of theater.

Now on a familiar platform, my stride lengthened, and I felt taller, more confident. Marcus, stationed at the light board, explained, "I need help getting the lights adjusted to look right on the red fabric."

I glanced over where he pointed to a red velvet fainting couch, an interesting choice for a burlesque act. Fainting couches are symbols of Victorian sexual repression. A burlesque act on this article of furniture would be subversive in a historical context.

I stood behind him and placed my hand on his shoulder as he reminded me of the function of the buttons and sliders. He moved behind and explained, "The red cloth absorbs the red light and appears white." He reached around my waist to slide a lever, and I turned my face toward his as he did toward mine. His warm breath caressed my cheek as he said, "I will sit as you try corrections."

He backed up a step, a little awkward, hesitant, and seemed reluctant to leave. But he walked over, sat, and spread out. I adjusted the levels, and his white t-shirt went from red to pink under the light. "You might remove your top so we can view the light on flesh tones," I suggested.

"I am far more interested in getting the light right on the seat," he reminded me as, in one easy motion, he lifted the shirt by the hem, up and over his head. When he tossed the shirt, it draped over the end of the seat. Topless in soft, blue denim jeans, Marcus reclined, half-naked and barefoot. If he wore no underwear, and he may not, he had on only one garment. Two less than most burlesque performers. And he did not even wear shoes.

I made a few adjustments, observing the red light on his glowing skin. I recalled Marcus was more concerned with the upholstery and proposed we trade places again. He rose, and I strolled from the light controls, passing him between.

Right before I reached the settee, I raised my hand to unhook a chain. The weight of the metal pulled the cloth over one breast. I turned to see widened eyes, parted lips, Marcus not moving.

I stood facing him for a moment, enjoying his attention and excited by my own boldness. Lowering myself, lying back on the soft seat in little more than half my attire, I knew I resembled an Egyptian, like Cleopatra.

Cleopatra is one of a long list I compiled of strong women leaders. Women maligned and murdered by men seeking domination of the civilized world, wresting it from strong women leaders. Cleopatra was not murdered, the threats of capture forced Cleopatra to commit suicide with her entourage of maid-servants.

I focused on my toes to give Marcus freedom to watch me and felt his gaze on my skin like my pores opened to absorb his attention. I glanced over to the curtain, still a half-meter open, but saw only the glow of the red fabric in the bright light, nothing in the darkness beyond.

In a moment the light changed, like a sudden sunrise, and I thought Marcus must have had the balance right. I thought he may have added another color to the mix. I marveled at my body and the golden skin tones on the bloom of the red velvet.

The red light poured over me, flooding onto the wood floor. A vision of Marie Antoinette came to mind. I envisioned gallons of red blood spilling out of her guillotined body, over the platform she knelt on and into the soil of the Place de la Revolution. I could smell the coppery scent of blood and feel the press of bodies crowding the square to witness the execution.

My thoughts careened back to Cleopatra, as her "needle," an ancient obelisk, stands over the place where Marie Antoinette lost her head. The gold pyramid pointed phallic *L 'Aiguille de Cléopâtre* rises from the ground in defiance of the men who forced her suicide.

Someone poked their head through the backstage door, "Curtains in twenty." Marcus and I said, "Thank you twenty," in unison and laughed together at the dramatic shorthand. Marcus, sure he had the lights right, wanted me to check and we traded places again. I moved to the panel as he walked back to the seat.

Passing between I detected the heat of his body. The energy emanating from him merged with my own coursing through me. In the nearness, I imagined hearing his heart beating like my own now pounding in my chest.

He reclined as I stood at the light board. One foot on the wood floor, grounding him, the other stretched out on the seat. There was no need for me to adjust the light—it appeared perfect. A red flood washing over his half-naked body, rich flesh tones, and the velvet glowing a deep reddish pink.

I knew whenever I moved, Marcus froze, and I did not give him time to rise before moving toward him from behind the controls. He stared, still as expected, his gaze screaming a question of what I would do next. He did not wait long to find out. Walking toward him I reached for the chain on the other shoulder. His eyes locked on my fingers as they unhooked the links. I paused and released, the dress fell to the floor.

I stepped out one foot at a time, like Alice Harford in the first scene of the movie Eyes Wide Shut. Unlike that scene, I faced him, now nude except for the red silk bow back panty and my glitter heels. Right in front of him, I turned to display the back. He may have seen the bow but I felt his attention on the cheeks of my bottom. His eyes moved to my thighs, the sensitive backs of my knees, pausing on my calves. The sensation like the lightest silk floating over my skin.

I turned and he stared into my eyes, his breath labored, he tried to speak. I smiled to acknowledge that words at this moment were unnecessary.

I placed my knee between his, knelt and leaned forward. My breasts were inches from his face, nipples hardening under his gaze. Elated and aroused, moisture began within me, as well as the sweat on my skin. Beads emerged on my brow and my mouth watered. I was sure he caught the aromas of sweat and essence, the pheromones of escalating passion.

I touched his lips with the tip of my finger and traced a line over his chin, continuing over his neck, chest, and belly. Pausing at his navel, I hooked the waist belt of his jeans and pulled, playful but determined. His eyes questioned, hoping for more direction. I lowered my head, smiled, and made a point to look down at my own insistent, tugging finger. He understood and unbuttoned and unzipped his jeans as I stood and moved back a step.

He slid his slacks down his thighs, calves, and over his feet almost in slow motion and he wore no underwear. Admiring his body, I thought of the curtain at least a few inches open, but I was entranced by his erection, begging engagement. His cock was large but not huge, a straight shaft terminating in a helmet head pulsing with arousal.

The artful lighting, his creation, washed over the glow of his skin. I lowered myself and placed a single finger on his cock. He flexed and in the flood of light the head swelled in response.

I stroked him; each caress raising him flexed off his belly. A final flex held him aloft as I wrapped my fingers around him and pulled toward me.

He stayed motionless, watching my hand wrapped around him, observing every movement. I also stared at my hand surrounding him. I stroked him toward me and pulled myself closer at the same time.

Our thighs met, smooth skin on smooth skin and I slid further until my knee pressed into him. He sighed and stared into my eyes, not knowing what to do with his hands. One found a place to rest on my belly, the other hand over mine on his own leg.

My hand slid over him with the lightest of strokes, each the full length. Sounds of the hall filling with an excited audience caught my attention. I almost diverted my gaze when he groaned in rapture and his head rolled back. My full attention returned to him. I released him to moisten my hand with saliva and closed my wet fingers over him, stroked the length once, twice, and once more.

Rhythmic contractions began against my knee as I pulled toward me and he began to climax. His breathing deepened, his muscles tautened, his toes pointed, his hips moved in synchrony with the climactic stroke. My fingers reached the head, I squeezed, and he arched his body. He came and came on my thigh, his warm semen flowing over my skin and dripping on the wooden floor.

I stared in wonder and curiosity as the viscid fluid, alive and glowing blood red, flowed from him over me and on the floor. I continued caressing him as he relaxed and melted back into the velvet.

With about five minutes left of our twenty, he reached for his t-shirt to clean me. He stopped when he realized I was rubbing the semen into my skin. He stared. Pleasant aromas of musk, mushrooms, his DNA, floated around us. My body aroused by the erotic energies and stimulated by these scents began tremors of orgasm coursing through me. Soft and tender at first building to an implosion. My body rocked with pleasure and I could not move.

I experienced what the French call *le petit mort*, the little death. I half sat, half knelt for a moment, still rubbing my thigh. Marcus stared in awe the whole time, then rose to dim the lights, shut the curtains all the way, and get ready for the beginning of the show. I rose and slipped back into my clothes, hooking the two chains. Marcus and I embraced, and he led me back toward my table. Stepping out and descending the stairway, I could feel him still watching me from the stage and I almost peered back.

My partner Rüdi would love this tale. Jealousy is not in our nature. We are not polyamorous, it is just that the bonding agents in our relationship include sexuality, but far more.

The hall was now crowded and Cat stood at my table with a fresh chilled glass, ready to pour. She had the best timing. I thanked her and sat down at my table and she stood by me as the music began. Horns and drums, woodwinds and strings, classical, though more like something crazy like Stravinsky.

The curtains opened on the Victorian fainting couch flooded with blood red light. Cat seemed transfixed, hypnotized as was, of course, I. The dancer entered in a formal metal-framed bustle. An elaborate bouffant hairstyle piled on the top of her head. Marie Antoinette. Earlier I must have somehow experienced the work of countless rehearsals on that red couch. It was certain she must detect the sexual scents of sweat and semen Marcus and I just left behind.

In usual burlesque style, she undressed in a well-choreographed tease. The dance ended as she reclined on the seat in no more than pasties and a thong; her hair still towering above. I wondered if Rüdi would count the hair as an article of clothing. But she did not run offstage. Instead, she stared out into the theater, at the audience. Her eyes scanned the faces of each guest, and then they fell on me.

She stared, like she recognized me. I heard my heart beat, like in the Edgar Allan Poe story, *The Telltale Heart*. Under her spell, recovering only when her eyes broke the stare, she and I glanced at Cat at the same time. Cat froze though her fingers danced on the table next to my glass. She was transfixed.

The music changed to a much more dramatic beat, and two gentlemen, garbed in fine robes, strode from both sides of the stage. One carried a platter with a huge slice of cake, the other a white cloth napkin and a fork. They offered these to her, and she took them from their hands before they departed in ceremony.

She moved the plate up to her nose but remained facing the audience. She breathed in the aromas and almost took a bite when the music changed again and two rude men in peasant garb, burst into view.

One of these men stole the plate from her hands as the other removed the elaborate hairdo from her in a ritualized act of decapitation. A slow-motion collapse and she feigned death, as the final part of her routine. She spread out, surrounded in a theatrical pool of blood.

The crowd went wild, shouting and clapping, hooting and hollering. They loved her, I loved her. The curtain closed like a waterfall of blood descending on the scene.

The falling red drapes ended the life and the performance of the now near naked Marie Antoinette.

Wild Release

Katherine S. Stafford

Having turned forty-five, I am about as midlife as you can be. At least I hope I'll live to ninety. I love my age and knew as a girl that I would blossom in my forties. Seems odd when culture projects our twenties—maybe thirties—as the height of our juiciness.

At a concert once, two men who seemed older than me—I was twenty-nine—approached me and one of their come-on lines was, "Did you know fifty is the new thirty?" I didn't know what to say at the time, though I didn't have to guess how old my suitors were. I thought about that again recently and realized that their formula would have put me at age nine. I mean, really?

So, I like forty-five as forty-five.

I earned those years. I don't want to go back to learning things the hard way—by swinging back and forth from one extreme to the next. I'm talking men, of course, but also my belief in myself. Sometimes I was full of ideas and adventure and then other times I would cling to desperation and depression as if I had no destiny. When I met my husband, I had turned my back on miles of uncompleted relationships, and in the end, I am grateful. I had to become my own woman before I could find my own man.

Fifteen years have easily flowed past, just as the constellations move predictably across the sky. Still, those glimmering patterns keep me in awe. I am in awe of my beloved husband who can flip the fluffiest pancake without losing a crumb then go out and swing an axe over his shoulder to cleave an oak log in two. I am in awe of my two sons, who say my laugh lines make me look happy and name my two deepest ones after themselves. I am in awe of where we call home, a comfortable ranch house on ten acres just outside of a friendly mountain town in Colorado. My very own constellation, making me feel that I am at the right place at the right time with the right people.

So, it took someone familiar to slip under the radar, like a satellite you get used to seeing passing through your sky every night. I was working on a historical fiction book with roots in my home state. Naturally, I looked to connect with a Colorado-oriented publisher. I was assigned an editor named Jason Braun out of Denver, about an hour-and-a-half drive from our hamlet, not that geography matters in our digital age. Our first exchanges were emails. Then he was the voice on the line, with questions, suggestions and deadlines.

Though technically my employer, Jason said things with such thoughtfulness and integrity that I forgot to keep my guard up. Or, maybe it was the midwestern accent—he is from the Twin Cities originally—that made him disarming, and I assumed, harmless.

By happenstance, we met for lunch once when I was in Denver on an errand run. I expected to meet a sandy colored man, doughy around the edges, with dewy eyes and horn-rimmed glasses. Instead, I was confronted with a quietly confident dynamism in literary wraps.

Jason sat in the booth with his long back hunched over a menu, black curly head of hair trying to point out various menu choices. I knew generally what he looked like from a staff photo on his company website, his mop of glossy black hair being his distinction. From the back I could not spy the horn-rimmed glasses he wore in the photo, but I noted the tailored shirt in a vibrant check that clung to his outline.

Surprising myself, in one glance I was drawn to his arms. I guessed those biceps could tell some stories, and the forearms showing below his rolled-up long-sleeves rippled like a flamenco guitar just holding the laminated menu. I was a bit relieved to see those bookish glasses when I slid into the booth opposite him.

"Oh, hello Becca!" The voice was him. The glasses were him, but the bodily shock of recognition I felt flow between us—that was not supposed to be any part of him. Without doing it consciously, I felt my upper back arch just slightly, so my breasts moved imperceptibly toward him. I noticed one corner of his mouth curl up just a bit, and his torso push into the edge of the Formica table with a steady, almost unnoticeable, pressure.

It was strange to talk shop, as indifferent as possible, with a man I suddenly felt naked in front of. Did he know I felt this way?

He must have, and he must have reciprocated the feeling. The more we talked about the book, the more double meanings kept slipping into our conversation. Finally, I just asked him, "Is there something more going on here?"

"Yes," he said. Simply, yes, and he looked straight at me, not one drip of dewiness in his steady, undistracted gaze. That is when I noticed the honey color of those eyes, fell in, and got stuck. But only briefly, struggling out like a lucky fly from a spider's web.

I ate denial for dessert. That is, I didn't stay long after that. I hustled me and my inappropriate—for so many reasons listed in my mind—attraction for my editor out of that booth and out to my car, trying to contain it with a slam of the driver side door. Contain it I did. I basked in that enjoyable, luxurious feeling of being wanted for the next two hours, barely noticing the traffic of rush hour that slowed me down on my way out of the city. I got to thinking about why we, responsible people like myself included, deny ourselves. Are we afraid that after choosing a path that has so defined us, in veering from it—not denying ourselves—we will lose ourselves? This self that others love, reinforcing the reasons to stay who we are? Or perhaps, we deny ourselves because we think that is what we deserve. Is it ingrained that the act of denial makes us noble, as in the religious sense?

I sat so still thinking, only my eyeballs moving to follow an occasional car or truck on the highway as I neared home, that my laugh lines nearly went flat in the rearview mirror. By the long gravel drive to our ranch house, I figured, mostly, it was about consequences.

If I eat this, it'll go to my thighs. If I don't meet this deadline, they won't want to work with me again. I started to see that what I thought were choices I was making were necessities of, or accommodations to, my already defined life. I began to feel a revolt within as a hollowing in my belly, a space for a scream to build. *To hell with societal expectations! I throw off my chains! I* thought wildly. It was about my liberty. I even felt righteous entertaining the thought of taking a lover.

Then my own voice from years ago, consoling my youngest who was worried about a silent birthday candle wish being heard, said in my mind, *sometimes wishes have a way of calling the fairies. They'll answer.* Had I, in some part of me, wished for this? Had I wished for that moment that transformed me from only me to a desirable and desiring woman?

My husband still wanted me, sometimes more than when we first met. We knew each other so well, knew how to please each other; there was never any doubt that we would be satisfied.

I love his body, his smell, his skill at pleasuring me to my extremes. We go there. When we kiss on an average day, in passing, we linger. Just the thought of my husband in this way and my heat will rise, and I know what will happen once the groceries are unloaded, dinner made and eaten, kitchen cleaned, kids in bed. Our bedroom door will be closed.

A few nights after the lunch with my editor I had nearly convinced myself that I had imagined the entire conversation. Perhaps I needed to write some good romantic fiction. My husband had driven to the neighbors to help them fix something broken, and the kids were tucked in bed. As usual, I was tidying up the kitchen from dinner and was starting to lay things out for the next morning. I heard a rustle and turned to see my seven-year-old son, Ben, in the doorway.

"Mom," he said, "my throat is dry, and well, I fell asleep, and I couldn't stop thinking about the bear that got into our garbage and whether it would come back. And then it was like it was in my room, a big shadow in the corner. And I said, 'I didn't invite you here,' and the bear just looked at me like it loved me." Then tears spilled out of his eyes and rolled down his cheeks, and I lunged to the floor to give him my special mama bear hug.

I kissed him on his warm, still downy cheek, "It's okay, baby. You're safe in your house with your Mama. I won't let the bears in." We cuddled for a moment, and then he shuffled off to bed.

I was moments alone, and my cell chimed. I use the bells as a way to center myself before I answer the phone, which tends to throw me off kilter. When I saw my editor's name flash on the screen, I needed centering more than ever. I tapped the green circle to answer, as nonchalantly as possible, then heard his greeting. Hearing his voice, his intonations blew my battened hatches wide open, leaving me, in the midst of my own kitchen, defenseless and adrift in an ocean of wanting.

That woman who drove back from Denver with a wild mind found herself marooned in my kitchen, on the center stage of family life. She felt out of place. She wanted to see his face as he spoke. I wanted to sprawl across his lap and murmur about the days past and the days ahead. Irrationally, I wanted to explore those feelings with him, yet, without parallel universes, this could never happen. I would not let it happen. I had not wanted an escape hatch, I was happy in my life. I had never once thought that there was another path for me.

Until that day.

Until Jason wasn't the bookish editor I thought he would be—bookish, yes, and restrained, his muscular body seeming to hold something in. In a word, smoldering. I went into Shakespeare's woods and down the rabbit hole, and though I hadn't eaten the apple that day, I knew I wanted to taste it.

"Hey, Jase," I murmured into my phone.

"Hey, Becca. Wait 'til you hear this. Are you ready for this?"

"Hopefully. It's good news?" I queried.

"Hope so. I'll be in your neck of the woods this weekend."

"Really? Oh my god. Really?" I sounded incredulous, but what I was feeling was anything but unbelieving. I got a thrill as if I were eight again and it was announced that it would be Christmas every day, starting this weekend. It hit me that this was the long weekend my husband flew to Seattle with the kids to see his family, a yearly tradition. When we have the money I go, too, but when we are tight, I stay home with one of the kids. This year we had enough airline miles that both kids could go.

I would be alone.

The fates had conspired.

Oh, lord.

Shit!

Life is part intention and part dealing with what falls into your lap. You make choices and then what happens, happens. This was happening. We decided to meet up, a first. Was this happening? I felt like another woman, his woman, and something in me more long-seeing knew that our coming together was as inevitable as the sun rising. Still, my thoughts tumbled in one after the other like waves pounding the shore of my conscience. Could I possibly have two places I belong? Here with my family and there with Jason? Is there a way of weaving them together? Or am I falling apart?

Oh my god, I'm having an affair.

But we haven't consummated it.

This is still an affair—these plans make it official.

I'm excited.

I'm despicable.

I'm selfish.

I'm human.

I'm alive.

I can't do this.

I will do this.

I want to do this.

I hear a motorcycle engine purr up the gravel road from the two-lane highway, dark and empty at this hour. Automatically, in nervous anticipation, I start doing some dishes. There are only two since only I had dinner at home tonight. I see the white flash of a headlight as it hits the living room window, then all is dark again. I hear the crush of pebbles under his riding boots as he dismounts his bike to mount my steps. I want to run, sprint to the door, fling it open. But I wait, grabbing the edge of the sink, feeling its cool, reassuring wetness. I feel a warm surge hit between my legs and I close my eyes, concentrating on the pleasure and the pain of it.

I am torn.

I am human.

I am woman, and tonight Jason is my man.

He knocks lightly, respectfully. I walk steadily to the door, remembering that these are my last moments of … what?

Not purity, I lost that long ago.

Domestication?

Pretension?

These are the last moments of the security of believing I know exactly who I am. Instead of feeling fear and pulling back within safe boundaries, I rush toward the ambivalence as if it were a brick wall between me and my freedom. Maybe this is who I have been all along.

There is no denying what this meetup is about. The image of Ben's bear flashes in front of me as I cross the living room of shadows. I shake my head once, then take the last step to the door, unlock it and pull the door open. There is Jason, and we are standing unmoving. The moonlight draws a silver line around his dark silhouette. He looks larger than he really is and projects the energy of a hungry animal. I smile knowingly instead of gasping. Then, we each take a half-step forward. We are close enough to feel the puffs of our breaths but far enough apart to meet each other's gaze in the silver light. The manmade smell of exhaust and fresh air wafts from his dark curly hair.

I don't know what we say besides hello, then he is across the threshold, and we are heading through the living room to the long hallway. I hear him close behind me, breathing hard from the exhilarating ride through the night, his unprecedented arrival at my door, and perhaps, his expectations. I want to smell him more, imprinting, so when we get to my bedroom door, I playfully push him ahead and inhale the air. This time warm leather, scalp sweat, and even the smell of cool condensation from the end of the day comes off of him. I smile at him, and he grins widely, his cheeks pinching in what looks like pure happiness. I know now that this is one-hundred percent genuine, his desire for me and his presence here. His eyes are watery from his ride. He is dewy and reborn, and all mine.

We step into my bedroom. I am glad only I slept in the bed last night, that only my smell lingers in the air. I am also glad it is dim, only lit by the light of the waxing moon through a window, and not light enough to define the faces in the picture frames on my dresser. Jason stands in front of me, filling my view, for which I am grateful.

That's when I notice his lack of glasses and tap my temple in a question.

"Contacts," he replies. "Glasses fog up in the riding helmet."

"Ah," I say. "What about the rest of your gear?"

I watch his hands, his precise hands, go to the industrial zipper of his leather riding jacket, tugging it down, while the corners of his mouth curl up sensuously. When all the padding comes off and he is standing in his t-shirt and jeans, I accept the invitation by twirling the shirt off over his head in one yank. His skin is pale under dark chest hairs, his nipples purple and erect, his muscular and yet malleable belly rapidly rising and falling.

I know where that masculine slope goes, and I grab his buckle, pulling his belt tight. He takes a sharp breath in and then I release the belt's tautness. His eyes are closed now, his head slightly cocked, his full lips and wide mouth in a meditative grin lifted toward the ceiling. I almost want to leave him there like that, in his anticipated transcendence, but I can't help but let the warmth from my groin guide my hand. I pop his jeans' brass button and slide down the zipper. His jeans need a little push to get around the round of his butt, then they crumple to the ground, along with any reluctance I have left.

I gently push him back a couple steps to sit on the edge of my bed, and I slide off his jeans along with his boots and socks. One boot hits the hardwood floor with a thud, sounding decisive and bold. The second boot gets caught on his heel and we laugh, breaking our trance. We get to looking at each other, and I remember how lucky we are to be here, and I feel grateful to be with this nearly naked man who clearly wants me. I leave him in his briefs and peel off my layers.

When I get down to my bra and panties, I feel the exquisite pressure of material on nipples, breasts, hips, and ass. It tantalizes me, but I also want them shed. He reads me and reaches around to my bra hook, brushing my upper arms with the tender, warm insides of his. His breath is humid on my neck as the hook releases and my bra falls open to the floor.

I barely feel the brush of my nipples on his chest before he is kneeling to mouth my nipples and breasts. I feel his fingers going around the elastic of my panties in the crotch, and his two fingers run lightly along the lips of my vulva. Slippery wetness coats his fingers as they probe gently. Already breathing rapidly, I groan when his fingers lengthen inside my vagina and are engulfed by my lips. He licks my belly button with a warm, wet tongue. I feel more animal than human, a moist creature. All I register is wetness and warmth and wanting. With one dry hand and one wet hand he slides off my panties, and his nose, lips, mouth, and chin dive into the warm depths of my pussy. He dives in and licks all the way up to my clit, throbbing and engorged. I moan.

He spins me gently around to the bed, so my bare ass sits on the cool cotton covers. I part my legs as I lean back and he buries his face back into my pussy, licking short and quick then long and slow. My breasts quiver and bounce as I arch my neck and back and shimmy my hips in response to his licks and sucks. I can't remain quiet, and I grunt and hum as the coil of lust tightens in my body. I throw my head back as a final howl marks my orgasm. I hold back nothing.

He doesn't let me slide away. His face follows my pelvis down as it releases tension, sinking into the billows of the sheets, and he licks tenderly, slowly at my clit. I quiver, hypersensitive, with each lick, but don't push him away. With this titillation, I want him in me. I flip over onto my belly and rise to my elbows and knees just enough so my nipples brush the sheets. I reach around with one hand and guide his projecting cock into my wet pussy. I feel his head pop in and I guide just his head in and out. My pussy tightens around his head. He grabs me by the hips and slides his penis in deeper with every stroke inward. I flick and rub my swollen clit, and I groan with the pleasure of his cock and my finger. He hits my g-spot and then keeps aiming for the spot with his thrusts. My tits are rocking front to back. His balls hit my pussy when he lunges forward.

He comes in me. I feel the extra pulses of his cock while he stays firmly within. He gives a throaty, groaning exhale. We fall forward onto the bed, and then spoon, basking in the after moment and our fresh sweat. I didn't quite come when he did, so I relish the feel of his cock as it slides out of me, retreating to its normal size. I don't want to lose our physical connection—I am still pulsing with energy, wanting more. I lay him on his back and sit my wet pussy on his abdomen. I finger myself with him watching, something I would never have done with my husband, feeling the self-consciousness of self-pleasuring, and fearing I would make him feel unneeded somehow. I work myself up as Jason intently watches, eyes still hungry. I don't care. It even turns me on more.

Feeling free, doing things I have never done before, I hear myself tell him I want him up my ass. I get a pleasant chill of speaking the forbidden after I say this. Nestled at rest between my ass cheeks, I feel his dick quiver. He has more hardness in him. I get back on my elbows and knees. I ask him to slap my ass, and he does with a satisfying slap. He dips his dick in my pussy for lube, which had gushed with the smack, then I start to feel the tip of his cock nudging my anus. I gasp with the unfamiliar pain mottled with pleasure of the opening of this place. He hesitates. I lean on one shoulder and cheek on the mattress and reach around to spread my ass. "Ah-hmm," I assent.

He starts to nudge, and I feel my sphincter give way to his head. He gradually massages his entirely enhardened cock up my ass. I rub my clit and angle my butt to his thrusts. The inside of my ass becomes juicy, and I ask him to hit me harder. I hear him grunting a little, and I cry out in response. Everything is rocking and smacking, stroking and nudging. Then we both tense, cry out, and release.

Cum is dripping out of my pussy and my ass. Still on my knees with my head down on the bed, I look past my shoulder and see his form smoldering like smoke behind me. We have performed magic I didn't know existed. A kind of transfiguration has occurred. I don't feel bound by my skin, which pulses and mingles with the air particles around it. I don't remember who I am, how old I am, or what I am, just that I am—feeling the reverb of coupling carnal and spiritual satisfaction.

When I wake up the next morning, sun streaming in the window, all is clear. The faces of my family on the dresser, where my skin ends and the sheets begin, and the strangeness of the situation is all present. There is no hangover, just reality. Jason, my editor, is in deep slumber beside me. The hot bulk of his body and his billowing hair at my back feels everything like a bear pelt. I have let the wild into my bed. I roll onto my belly to my other side so I can study him. With my shifting he has moved onto his belly with his head buried in his arms, crossed above his head, so all I see is his hair in a mound of glossy shag. I tousle it like I would a dog between the ears, and he attempts to raise his head. His syrupy eyes peep open for a moment before they close again, and his head drops back into his arms. I let my hand run down his spine and follow the rise of his coccyx bone to his lightly furred bum. Patting it, I slip from the bed and head for the shower.

As usual, the morning rush of a warm shower puts my molecules in place and in motion for the day. Donning a robe, I head back into the bedroom to see Jason up and dressed. I am glad he doesn't seem to want to linger, and I sense that he is only minutes from being on the road. He almost seems in rewind as he zips up his leather jacket and heads for the door without a word. He isn't rushed, he just knows the right time to make an exit.

We stand at the threshold once more, lingering a moment, breathing each other. Then he pivots and looks out at his bike, chrome gleaming in the morning sunlight. He takes a step toward it, then pauses and glances back. And there it is, a look like love.

I smile until the door comes between us, like a final curtain. With a turn of a lock, the wildness is gone.

Contributors

Amelia Allende

Amelia is working on a collection of short stories about broken things, including bodies, children, faith and love.

She comes from a Northern Nevada Spanish Basque family and is a special needs mom and advocate. She runs a policy consulting company that specializes in social innovation in Reno, Nevada.

Amilia holds an MA in Political Science from Washington State University and is a past Women's Research and Education Institute Fellow. Her stories can be found in "Cagibi" and "The Spectacle."

She lives in Reno, NV, with her husband and three children.

Caycie Thompson

Caycie Thompson is a writer of erotic fiction in Ontario.

Check out her website, cayciethompson.com, for daily writing prompts for writers of erotica and sexy short stories.

She can be found on Twitter and Instagram at @writtenbycaycie.

Gina Durden

A Carolina girl transplanted West who brought the South with her in the form of sensuousness and curiosity. Who forbids us? Most of the time we forbid ourselves out of fear or misunderstanding. Breaking free of such self-administered limitation is one of the great victories of a lifetime.

Gina writes to explore the wonder and diversity of all forms of loving. And they are copious and everywhere.

Grüdier

Grüdier is an emerging fiction writer. He has written extensively for websites and has been published in commercial, spiritual, and psychological journals.

Energy and energy science are overriding themes in his writing. Grüdier is currently working on a book of short stories, featuring Cosette, a character undergoing transformation through erotic adventure.

Katherine S. Stafford

Katherine S. Stafford lives with her family of four in the Lost Sierras of California. A graduate of UC Santa Cruz in American Studies and Columbia University School of Nursing in Nursing Science, she likes to use both sides of her brain, but not without first consulting her heart.

Besides dabbling in erotica, and enjoying it, she is also working on her first book, *Love on Many Fronts*, a creative memoir and love story based in modern wartime.

Concurrently she is looking to publish a poetry collection spanning thirty years of her life called *Back Forty*.

Patrick Bruskiewich

Patrick is a Canadian born, Vancouver writer. He enjoys short stories and particularly short stories that speak to the beauty and aesthetics of art and the human condition.

This story, "Imagine …" is based on a real–life encounter from almost two decades ago. The art history student in this story had never experienced the dichotomy of the human condition. It is for that reason she chose to study the Male Form in the Classical World as part of her art history course.

Unlike the cold and ancient stone sculptures in the Roman and Greek section of the Metropolitan Museum, in her world, Patrick became a living sculpture for her to study.

Patrick understands she received an A+ as her term project mark.

Other Works from Temptation Press

Summer Fling

Kiss & Tell

The Professor

Private Lessons

Choices

This Sub's for You

Intimate Moments

A Note from the Publisher

How to Thank a Contributor

Dear Reader,

Everyone at Temptation Press would like to thank you for reading *Forbidden: An Erotic Collection of Short Stories*. If you would like to thank a particular contributor, the best way is to leave a review for them. You may do so by leaving one on our Goodreads page, under the title, *Forbidden*, by using the link below:

http://www.goodreads.com/TemptationPress

and be sure to mention the contributor directly.

Why should you leave a review? Reviews help budding authors build their credibility in the book industry. By posting a review on Goodreads and other review sites, you help other readers find new authors they may wish to follow, and you never know, your review may end up on an author's website one day.

Friend us on Goodreads:
https://www.goodreads.com/TemptationPress

Visit our website:
http://www.TemptationPress.com

www.ingramcontent.com/pod-product-compliance
Lightning Source LLC
Chambersburg PA
CBHW061533050726

47593CB00002B/769